Taking the Temptress

EM BROWN

ISBN-13: 978-1-942822-07-3

A GENTLE WARNING

This novel contains BDSM elements, themes of
submission and dominance, and many other
forms of wicked wantonness.

OTHER WORKS BY EM BROWN

For more about these wickedly wanton stories,
visit www.EroticHistoricals.com

GOT HEAT?

"Ms. Brown has written a tantalizing tale full of hot sex…a very sexy and sometimes funny read that will definitely put a smile on your face."

– Coffee Time Romance review of
AN AMOROUS ACT

"Darcy's fierce, independent spirit and unconditional loyalty to her family will win readers over, and Broadmoor is a romantic hero to swoon for."

- RT Book Reviews on
FORCE MY HAND

"Sometimes you just pick up the right book that just hits you and makes you really love it. This was one of those books for me. I just got so into the story and never wanted it to end."

- Romancing the Book review of
SUBMITTING TO THE RAKE

"HOT AND FUN TO READ!!!!!!!!"

- Reader review of
ALL WRAPPED UP FOR CHRISTMAS

"This one made me go WOW! I read it in a few hours which technically I probably should have gotten more sleep, but for me it was that good that I deprived myself of sleep to finish this most awesome story!"

"…sex was intense…thrilling…."

"I loved this book. Clever dialogue that kept m[e] laughing, delightful characters and a wonderful story. I am not generally one who likes historical fiction but this book carried me along from page one."

Taking the Temptress

Chapter One

Holding her down, he thrust himself into her. Terrell thrust back, in part to meet his cock as it drilled into her but mostly to keep her hips from grinding uncomfortably against the back of the settee. Master Gallant would have been mindful of her discomfort. There was little he would have been unaware of. He was unlike most men she knew.

Sir Arthur exemplified her better understanding of his sex. Such men would pleasure a woman to arousal, ready her cunnie, and once they had entry and were given to the throes of their own pleasure, all else was forgotten. Once they had finished, the likelihood they would attend to her needs diminished to nothing.

In her mind, Terrell traveled from the room she was always assigned with Sir Arthur to the room upstairs, where she and Master Gallant had last occupied. She could not stop recalling their last moments in bed together, how he had twice taken her, how his every touch made the arousal flow between her legs, how firmly he had held her down upon the bed, holding that exquisite release at bay till the desperation mounted enough to catapult her into the heavens of carnal ecstasy.

Every moment thereafter had also satisfied. She had relished the sensation of his seed inside her. Though she would have preferred not to be barren so that one day, should she desire a little one of her own, the prospect would be hers, she took solace in not requiring the use of condoms and that she need never worry of conceiving an unwanted bastard. For a fleeting moment she had the strange notion that she would not mind carrying the child of Master Gallant. But as kind as his nature might be, his sex had another nature when confronted with a bastard. She had seen enough men treat women with all affection, then cast them aside with repugnance, wanting nothing to do with the child.

Sir Arthur began to heave and grunt, slapping his groin at her fast and furious. Her skirts, thrown up over her back, slid down and nestled between them. She knew him to be nearing his climax and clenched her cunnie down upon him. Seconds later, he wailed and shuddered. She flexed her cunnie once more.

"No—cease," he gasped, his member too sensitive.

When he had withdrawn, she turned to face him and went down to her knees. She threaded her fingers through the hair of his pelvis. He gasped, no doubt fearing she might touch his now limp shaft. She rubbed her hands about the area of his jewels.

"We have time for a second bout," she said and licked the underside of his sack.

He shivered.

Staring at his shrunken shaft, she said, "I hunger for this marvelous weapon, this sword you wield with such force."

"Alas, it is better I go," he said.

"Are you certain?" She sucked one of his cods into her mouth.

"Wanton wench." He pushed her away and reached for his handkerchief.

"Allow me, Sir Arthur."

She licked his cock, then took it into her mouth. He

shivered once more, staring at her with widened eyes. Cleansed, he replaced his member and buttoned his fall. He shook his head.

"Where must you head this evening?" she asked, hoping he would not have opportunity to return to the inn later tonight, as he had once done, surprising her and Master Gallant as they stood conversing in the hall. She expected Master Gallant at the Red Chrysanthemum in two hours' time.

"I am to travel to Dressex on the morrow."

"Dressex? Where is that?"

"In Somerset."

She tried to hide her excitement and pouted. "That is exceedingly far. Why must you trouble yourself to travel such lengths?"

"A friend, Lord Beggington, has some of the finest hunting grounds in all of England."

Watching him adjust his cravat in the mirror, she stood and leaned against the settee. "You are choosing hounds and deer over my company? For certain you will be gone at least a sennight."

"Ten days."

"There is sufficiently fine hunting nearer to London."

He turned to look at her and smiled. She would rather he did not, for his smiles always bore a sinister quality.

"Will you miss my person or my coin?"

She sidled up to him. "Your *cock* and your coin."

He inhaled sharply. "Are all blackamoors as lascivious as you?"

"Say, rather, that no one is as wanton as me. Will you not choose a more convenient destination?"

"Lord Beggington owns several boroughs that he might wish to part with. I intend to make him an offer he cannot refuse."

"Do you not own enough, including Porter's Hill?"

He reached for his coat and slid his arms into the sleeves. "Porter's Hill is not quite in my pocket, but I own enough of it that I can sway an election."

She kept her eyes lowered as she buttoned his coat. "And have you selected whom you will support?"

She felt his careful gaze upon her.

"You have an interest in Porter's Hill?"

"I understand Mr. Gallant seeks to represent the borough."

"Did he tell you that?"

She heard the edge in his voice and remembered what Lady Sarah had said of his temperament.

"There are few secrets here at the Red Chrysanthemum," she deflected.

He grasped her hands as she finished the last button. "Ten days is indeed a long time. I would I did not have to leave, but I know I am not the only one interested in the boroughs Lord Beggington owns. If I could return earlier, I would."

She met his stare. "Then make it so. I have no doubt you will succeed at whatever you endeavor."

"And when I return, will you be waiting for me?"

"Madame will not wish me idle while I am quartered here."

"How much is your rent?"

"My rent takes the form of my, er, services."

"I will make it worth your while—and hers—to be idle. I do not wish for you to service anyone while I am away."

"I am certain an arrangement can be made. Madame strives to accommodate the membership."

"I will speak to her tonight then."

His eyes bored into her, and she felt once more that odd unease that had shivered her to the bones her first time with Sir Arthur.

"You will not entertain any man," he pronounced grimly, his hands tightening painfully about hers.

"What of women?"

"I suppose I can grant you the fair sex—provided you reprise your activities for my pleasure upon my return."

She smiled. "I should be delighted, Sir Arthur."

"Please me and you shall be amply rewarded. Cross me and you will dearly wish you had not."

Surprised by the intense, almost wild quality in his eyes, she said nothing.

He gave her a shake. "Do you understand, Miss Terrell?"

"Perfectly," she said.

"Good."

When he was gone, she let out a relieved sigh. She wondered if she ought to continue with the man, but his coin was far too rich. Madame Devereux, proprietress of the den of wicked desires, would not wish her to desist. Sir Arthur was the wealthiest patron the Red Chrysanthemum had ever seen. If Terrell could amuse Sir Arthur a while longer, she might save enough such that she would not need the Red Chrysanthemum any longer. She could secure her own lodgings and perhaps find more suitable employment if she required funds. Though she had long grown accustomed to the use of her body to satiate the desires of men, the freedom from whoring held much appeal.

But leaving the Red Chrysanthemum meant leaving Master Gallant.

Terrell made her way back to her own room, the new

one Madame had rewarded her for her assistance in the instruction of Lord Wendlesson's wife, Miss Katherine. Though the smallest room available to members, it was far more spacious than the prior space in the attic, where one could not stand without bending one's head to avoid the low and slanted roof.

She surveyed the new quarters with satisfaction. The room had a window and a fireplace. For that reason, she had invited Miss Sarah to join her in the new quarters. With the weather growing cooler, Terrell did not wish for Miss Sarah or the little one to suffer the cold nights of the coming winter. And she enjoyed their company. Little George might be the closest she would ever come to having a babe of her own.

She walked to the sideboard and poured water into the basin. She wished to cleanse herself of Sir Arthur before Master Gallant arrived. From the tenor of their last dialogue, she doubted she would be invited to attend his fifth lesson with Miss Katherine. She could find a way to inveigle herself into the instruction, and perhaps it was possible Lord Wendlesson, would still have an interest in her presence, but Master Gallant had held out the possibility of accepting her as his submissive if she adhered to his request. And she wanted to prove that she could please him, that she could be the best submissive he had ever had.

Wiping her thighs drew her attention to the area between. How was it his caresses could be so potent, eliciting the most divine sensations and driving her to distraction? Even her own hands did not seem to carry the efficacy of his. She touched herself to confirm her own assessment. Closing her eyes, she remembered how, lying upon her back, his weight had pressed the length of her into the bed, how he had buried himself inside of her, how his groin had ground against her rump. She wondered if he would ever take her arse. The thought sent heat rippling through her loins, and she rubbed herself faster.

It would be no easy task to keep her hands to herself in his presence, especially when reading the naughty and salacious work of Mr. Cleland. She was a little surprised Master Gallant had agreed to read to her when he had rebuffed all her other pleas. He was not immune to her charms. Of that she was certain. Of his stated objections for why he would not indulge in taking a submissive who could bring him the finest corporal pleasures, she was less convinced. She understood that he had no wish to vex Sir Arthur, whose support he wanted for his upcoming election, but they need only proceed with caution. It was easily possible to keep their affair secret, especially now that Sir Arthur would be gone for over a sennight.

As for his other remonstrance, she had suspected his partiality to Mistress Scarlet from the beginning. The depth of his feelings for the redhead surprised Terrell, but Madame doubted Mistress Scarlet to ever return to the Red Chrysanthemum.

Chapter Two

I am being removed as Miss Katherine's instructor?" Charles Gallant inquired in disbelief as he stood before Joan's writing table in the room that served as her office. After the progress made last night—with the assistance of Miss Terrell—he failed to understand Joan's course of action.

"I thought you would be relieved," the proprietress replied.

"That depends. Who will take my place?"

"I will."

Charles turned around to see that Lord Wendlesson had entered the room. The man seemed more at ease than he had on prior occasions.

"I am glad to hear it," Charles said, though he harbored a modicum of reservation.

"That is what you wanted from the start, was it not?" Wendlesson asked.

"Indeed. I hope, however, that you will be gentle and patient with her. She has made great strides, but your experience far exceeds hers."

"Worry not. I had believed, mistakenly, that I required more from my wife. You have inspired me, Master Gallant, with your approach. I confess I have a heavier hand, but I will endeavor to emulate you as much as possible."

"I am certain Miss Katherine will be elated with her

new instructor."

"She seemed pleased," Wendlesson acknowledged with a smile, "and eager to begin her lesson tonight. I ought not keep her waiting but did wish to offer my heartfelt gratitude for your service, as well as this."

The viscount presented a sealed letter. "If you wish to make use of it, it is a letter of introduction to my cousins, the Brentwoods. You refused any compensation or reward for your efforts, but I should be pleased to recommend your candidacy for their support."

Charles looked at the letter without accepting it. "I appreciate the recommendation, Lord Wendlesson, but my activities here have no bearing on my abilities to serve in Parliament."

Wendlesson grinned. "On the contrary, I think a good number of Members of Parliament merit a good disciplining."

"No doubt," Charles allowed with a partial smile, "but I have already applied for a meeting with your cousins."

"And have they granted you a meeting?"

"No."

Wendlesson presented the letter once more. "Then take this. My cousins are known for their generous support of candidates they endorse, but I think they have taken little action as of yet because Mathilda has had to attend to a family affair. I do not foresee, however, that they will remain dispassionate in this election."

After a brief hesitation, for he was loath for his membership at the Red Chrysanthemum to intersect with any other part of his life, Charles accepted the letter. He had sought a meeting with the Brentwoods for some time without success. His father, who had sought the burgess of Porter's Hill thrice, and thrice lost, believed that he would have won if the Brentwoods had supported him.

"I speak true," Wendlesson continued, "when I say that you would make a fine MP. Your skills here at the Red Chrysanthemum notwithstanding, I can see that you have much to recommend you: intellect, integrity, and other qualities I believe will stand you in good stead with your peers."

Thinking of Sir Arthur, Charles was tempted to dispute the viscount. Instead, he said, "You flatter me, my lord."

"I do not flatter lest it is true. I am much obliged to you."

"In regards to the instruction of your wife, Miss Terrell had an equal if not greater hand in her progress."

"And she has been amply rewarded for her assistance," Joan interjected. "At your suggestion, I have installed her and, at her request, Miss Sarah and her son in a brand new room."

"Which one?"

"A very nice room at the end of the hall upon the third floor."

Charles suspected it was the second smallest room to be had in the Inn, but he was glad to hear that Miss Terrell no longer shared a room in the attic.

"The assistance of Miss Terrell was invaluable," Wendlesson concurred. To Joan, he asked, "I would like to call upon her services again if I require it."

An unexpected wave of jealousy overcame Charles. He felt his jaw tighten. "I believe Miss Terrell spoken for."

"Are you referring to Sir Arthur?"

"Yes." Charles looked to Joan. "And I believe Sir Arthur had certain requirements of Miss Terrell."

Joan pursed her lips. "Yes, well…"

Charles knew Joan wished to please both Sir Arthur

and Lord Wendlesson, but there was no splitting of the babe this time, as she had attempted to do with Miss Lily, a young submissive who had unwittingly provided him the opportunity to claim the woman he had most desired— Mistress Scarlet.

"I hesitate to trespass upon his *generosity* further," Charles said, expecting Joan to weigh the purses of each men and find Sir Arthur's to be the heavier one. "He is not a man who will take lightly to having his expectations foiled."

"True, true. He did reiterate to me this very evening his desire to have Miss Terrell all to himself."

"But she would not be—I would not be making use of her, so much as my wife, who finds great comfort—and titillation—in her presence," objected Wendlesson.

"The best laid intentions can be thwarted by the passions of the moment," Charles said to the viscount, remembering the night Wendlesson had availed himself of Miss Terrell when he could not find his conclusion with Miss Katherine.

Of course, Charles was himself guilty of succumbing to Miss Terrell's charms. Not once. But several times. He could blame the first encounter on her. The blackamoor had conceived a most outrageous scheme to force his arousal. His body had never felt so violated.

Nor so aroused.

He found the assigning of fault to be almost always an endeavor that bore no fruit. He knew he was not innocent of blame. Nevertheless, if she had not forced herself upon him, he might not have found himself sliding down that forbidden slope. But having tasted of her in the most intimate manner in which a man might know a woman corporally, he could not resist taking her again. And again.

Her cunnie had been every bit as marvelous as she had boasted. He wondered that he could abstain from revisiting that piece of heaven, but he had resolved to do so and had told her as much last night before they parted.

"I myself," Charles continued, "have found forbearance difficult. Our sex is weak in this respect."

"'Tis true," Joan said. "Eve is far too great a temptation for Adam. In truth, he never stood a chance. I think it best we refrain from calling upon Miss Terrell."

Now that he had blocked Wendlesson's requests, Charles wondered if the man wished for his letter of introduction back. He wanted to add that Miss Terrell could prove as much a distraction as a benefit and that Miss Katherine would benefit from having the whole attention of her husband.

"I firmly believe that Miss Katherine no longer requires Miss Terrell," Charles said to the viscount. "*You* are all that she needs and all that she desires."

After a momentary frown, Wendlesson straightened. "I must add foresight, modesty, and forthrightness to Master Gallant's many commendable qualities. I hope you will make use of my letter."

With that, he bid them good night to attend to his wife. After he had departed, Joan let out a sigh.

"I thought for certain he would pursue the matter more," she said. "He is a man accustomed to having his way, and I'd be in quite the bind having to choose between him and Sir Arthur. You indeed work magic, Charles."

Wendlesson knew that Charles had knowledge of his lordship's congress with Miss Terrell, and Charles suspected *that* played more a part. Though Wendlesson had sought relief with Miss Terrell that night, Charles believed the man truly wished to improve the situation with his wife.

"You may credit his devotion to her ladyship," he said instead, "but I will involve myself no more betwixt a married man and woman."

"You need not worry. You have fulfilled our arrangement, and I release you from your servitude."

Charles took in a deep breath at his newfound freedom. Not that his obligation weighed upon him in any terrible form; he had readily agreed to her proposal—to serve her any purpose—if he could not win Miss Greta. Granted, he had been convinced at the time that he would prevail. Though Greta had chosen neither him nor Master Damien, fleeing instead to Liverpool with no indications of ever returning to the Red Chrysanthemum, Charles had honored his end of the bargain with Joan.

"And you were convinced it would not happen with Miss Katherine," she said. "*I* had more confidence in your abilities than you did."

"Hubris led to my failure with Miss Greta," he replied. "I did not intend to make the same mistake a second time."

"And I warned you there, did I not? Though you had made as much headway with Mistress Scarlet as anyone could, it simply was not meant to be."

He disagreed. Though Greta had assumed the identity of Mistress Scarlet for some time, he believed she had done so to escape the pain that Master Damien had inflicted upon her. Greta was, at heart, a submissive. Charles was certain he had been on the cusp of reviving Miss Greta when Master Damien, after an absence of several years, made a surprise reappearance.

Joan put on her spectacles and reviewed a list upon her writing table. "I expect Miss Lily to be here tonight. You remember the fair young nymph? She is without a constant Master or Mistress. I would be happy to pair you with her. I have no doubt she would be overjoyed to be with you again."

He shook his head. His interest in Miss Lily had only extended as far as a means for obtaining the attention of Greta. "I think I will take a respite whilst I attend to the election."

Joan furrowed her brow. "But you are barely returned to the Red Chrysanthemum and have spent so little time here since your lengthy travels to the Orient. With your seniority, you have your pick of any member."

Miss Terrell came to mind, but he dismissed the thought as quickly as it had come. As he himself had underscored, Miss Terrell was spoken for.

"I would you enjoy yourself, *mon cheri*. Will you not celebrate your achievement with Miss Lily, or any member to your liking, as the prize?"

"I will stay tonight, but not because I intend to claim a prize. As I owe my success with Miss Katherine to Miss Terrell, I had promised to read to her from *Fanny Hill*."

Joan wrinkled her nose. "Read? To Miss Terrell?"

He smiled, recalling how the passage from that naughty novel had aroused all in the room. "Mr. Cleland is perhaps equally responsible in the instruction of Miss Katherine."

"He is a brilliant writer, though I myself prefer the works of de Sade."

"De Sade would have terrified Miss Katherine, and I would hazard Miss Terrell's abilities with the French language to be limited."

"I would hazard nonexistent, but she asked you to read to her as recompense for her assistance?"

"I believe her satisfied with the reward you had

provided."

"Nevertheless, she is not one to overlook the opportunity of a perquisite. A reading hardly satisfies. I wonder what she is up to?"

"She took to Mr. Cleland with great interest. Is that so difficult to believe?"

"I suppose not. Still…I should not be surprised if she is as interested in Mr. Cleland as she is with *you*."

He considered revealing that he had discovered Miss Terrell could not read, but it was not his place to disclose that which she had tried to keep unknown to him.

"Why would she take an interest in me when she has Sir Arthur to entertain? If Miss Terrell is as devoted to the coin as you imply, I hardly provide rich fields to plow."

"You have enough. Moreover, Sir Arthur is gone for ten days or more. I would be cautious if I were you. She may be up to some mischief."

"She does very well for you and the Red Chrysanthemum."

"Yes, and I never would have thought a blackamoor could do so. And to attract the attentions of a man like Sir Arthur! *Mon dieu*, I did not think it possible for a man to have the sort of wealth he does. Miss Sophia dared to be peevish with me, for she thought I always gave Miss Terrell the rich ones, but Sir Arthur requested Miss Terrell. Frankly, Miss Sophia has been a disappointment of late, though she is pretty, and I am certain she would do well enough as a Covent Garden lady. I told her as much."

Glad that the conversation had veered away from Miss Terrell, Charles replied, "I have had few dealings with Miss Sophia, but I expect she did not receive your comments well."

"She did not but recognizes that she has some standing

here. She would have to start at the bottom elsewhere."

Charles looked down at his letter. In his other hand, he held a small parcel. He looked forward to presenting it to Miss Terrell.

"If you do not require my services, I will take my leave," he said. "Frankly, I will be glad to return home at a decent hour tonight."

"Take care with Miss Terrell," she reminded him after he had bowed and prepared to take his leave. "I doubt Sir Arthur would look upon an innocent reading with pleasure. It is an *innocent* reading?"

As innocent as could be had when reading the ribald tale of Miss Fanny Hill, he thought to himself.

"I can handle Miss Terrell," he assured Joan.

But even as he spoke the words, he knew they were of limited truth. He could not deny a great curiosity to know her better. She surprised, mortified, and impressed him. He knew no person like her. If he was to be completely honest with himself, she alarmed him, too. He could not predict his reactions when he was with her. With a simple sway of her hips, she weakened his forbearance.

But he had resolved not to be swept into the maelstrom that was Miss Terrell. Disaster awaited.

On his way to the Red Chrysanthemum, he had passed the apothecary where Miss Greta had worked alongside her father. He had stopped in several times to inquire of her, hoping that he would obtain some information as to when she would return to London. Tonight, however, he had continued on. He was ready to put Miss Greta behind him.

And he would eventually do the same with Miss Terrell.

Chapter Three

"Master gallant is to read to me tonight, nothing more," Terrell said to Miss Sarah, with whom she shared a room. Terrell was certain her excitement glowed in her eyes and was glad for George to fixate upon. Miss Sarah's little boy held on to the bed, one foot tentatively in the air as he contemplated taking his first step. The space the two women had shared in the attic barely had room to breathe between the cots. Now they occupied a small room with the grand space of eleven inches between the beds.

"Merely reading?" Miss Sarah inquired with a raised eyebrow and half smile to indicate her doubt.

Terrell returned the impish smile. "Of course I would it much more, but he is hesitant to upset Sir Arthur."

"He is wise. Sir Arthur will not perceive your time with another man kindly."

Miss Terrell needed no reminding, and Miss Sarah had made known her concerns many times before.

"Sir Arthur is gone to Somerset for ten days," Terrell replied. "He departs tomorrow morning."

"Ah. How fortunate for you."

George put his foot down, deciding against the step.

"My husb—Sir Rowen," Sarah quickly corrected, "once told me he was near two years of age before he took his first step."

"Is he not still your husband? He has not secured a

divorce yet."

"No doubt he will pursue it when Parliament is back in session. He wishes for an heir and would not want our separation to prevent him from remarrying." Miss Sarah sighed. "If he could only see how much Georgie looks like him…"

Terrell looked between mother and son. Save for the wide brow, the flaxen-haired boy bore little resemblance to his mother. In many ways, they had contrasting features. Miss Sarah had dark brown hair, a slender, pert nose, and general slimness of figure. Already tall for his age, George projected to be stout and had very square features to his physiognomy.

George raised a chubby foot, again contemplating a step. Miss Sarah held her breath as it looked as if he might advance, but he promptly sat upon his arse. The two women laughed. Miss Sarah picked him up and tickled him.

Terrell marveled at the boy's delightful giggles. Fed and provided for, children seemed unaffected by their circumstances, blissful in their ignorance. George knew not he was deemed a bastard by his own father. He knew not the life he would not know, that instead of a fine home in Berkeley Square, he resided in an inn where patrons indulged in sinful, wicked desires. She recalled the babes that would lie near the plantations fields, sucking contentedly upon cane, seemingly mindless of the insects that would land upon them. They knew not they were born into slavery.

Every time she felt the emptiness of her womb and the pangs of being barren, Terrell reminded herself that she was grateful she would not bear a bastard. She would not bear a child into that awful institution and condemn it to a life of hardship. Though she had her freedom whilst she remained in England, she did not delude herself into thinking that a child of hers would necessarily know a life of happiness. If he were fortunate, her son might find work in a respectable trade and be able to provide for himself. But he would look at other men and wonder why his opportunities need always be limited.

George continued to laugh, and Miss Sarah seemed to share his pleasure. Her countenance brightened, and her eyes sparkled. Though Terrell was not without jealousy for what Miss Sarah possessed and she would never know, it pleased her to see Sarah happy. Miss Sarah did not deserve her current situation. Certainly George did not. While Miss Sarah had entertained the affections of another man, she had never committed the criminal congress the jury had deemed her guilty of.

Taking a seat on her bed, Terrell chose to enjoy the child's laughter. Looking down at her best gown, a faded muslin, she saw a spot where the fabric was beginning to tear. Not skilled with needle and thread, she dreaded repairing garments. She could change her attire for her custJonesy corset and petticoats, but she wanted to persuade Master Gallant that she could behave. She wanted to appear as much a lady—she had once been a courtesan to a Member of Parliament—as she could and not the coarse strumpet, the unrefined Negress, he no doubt thought she was, even if he never treated her as such.

"When are you to meet with Master Gallant?" Sarah asked, giving George a reprieve and setting him on her lap. He commenced playing with her hair.

"After his lesson with the Lady Wendlesson. I can hardly wait."

"Of all the men who have passed through the doors here, I think him the finest. Not because he is the most striking, though he is plenty handsome, but because I can find no fault in him. He is a proper gentleman in every regard."

Terrell was silent in agreement before saying, "If he had Sir Arthur's wealth, he would be perfection."

"Master Gallant is not without means. His family has breeding. Though the elder son went into the Navy, he is highly regarded in his position. Even Captain Gracechurch, who rarely dispenses admiration, speaks well of him."

"But the Gallants must be far from the wealth of Sir Arthur."

"Who is not? I have heard Sir Rowen comment many a time how he would not mind being called a nabob if he had Sir Arthur's fortune."

"I suppose I am a fool for thinking of anyone besides Sir Arthur."

Sarah gave her a sympathetic smile. "I understand the appeal of Master Gallant. I, too, witnessed his performance with Mistress Scarlet. *You* were a lucky doxy to be called to the stage."

Terrell could feel warmth blossoming below her waist as she recalled that fateful night that drew Master Gallant to her attention. She had seen him before and liked the look of him. His features were in extremely fine proportion, with long golden lashes fringing blue crystalline eyes, the sincerest eyes she had ever beheld in a white man. She admired the varied hues of his dark flaxen hair, his tailored clothing and well-tied cravat. The sight of his bare and chiseled, but not overly brawny chest had made her lick her lips.

But most of all, it was what he did that had made her wet between the legs. Before an audience of members at the Red Chrysanthemum, he had tamed the proud and hitherto indomitable Mistress Scarlet. He had such mastery and command. Terrell thought she could feel it on every inch of her skin. She had never seen anyone work such wonders with ordinary rope. She yearned to be trussed in the same manner in which he had bound Mistress Scarlet.

And then there was the kiss.

He had wanted to taste Mistress Scarlet upon her, for she had applied her mouth to the pale and slender redhead. Once his mouth had taken hers, Terrell cared not his reason for kissing her. The way in which he had savored her mouth had sent the blood rushing to her head. His mouth had led the dance between their lips, and she was content to follow. When at last he had relinquished her, she knew she wanted the man more than she had ever wanted any of his kind before.

With white men, she had only ever taken a mild interest in the venereal sense. Their purse was the attribute that most compelled her. It surprised her to find she could lust after him when she had only desired fellow blackamoors before.

"I wonder when his time here will come to an end." Miss Sarah mused.

"Come to an end?" Terrell did not like the thought.

"He may not have the affluence of Sir Arthur or the nobility of Lord Wendlesson, but there is much promise to his career as he is favored by his employer, Sir Canning. I expect his prospects for election to be quite good."

"The burgess he seeks is for Porter's Hill. Or is it Potter's Hill? No, it is Porter's Hill."

"Yes, you know of it?"

"I know Sir Arthur to boast he owns half the borough, among many others."

"That is unfortunate, but I expect Gallant could earn the man's support if he desired to."

"And you think once he is elected to Parliament, he will quit the Red Chrysanthemum? Sir Arthur is an MP, and not the only one to patronize the inn."

"Perhaps not. But I doubt Gallant will remain a bachelor for long."

"When has marriage stopped a man from pursuing his venereal fulfillment?"

"True. Somehow, and this be speculation on my part, for I know Gallant little, he seems a different sort of man."

Terrell had thought the same. Perhaps that was what also drew her to him, not just his masterful abilities with rope bondage. As much as he had once infuriated her before by trussing her to the rafters and leaving her to hang in solitude for half an hour, he had aroused in her an even greater determination to have him claim her.

He had said, on more than one occasion, that she was too willful, too disobedient to be a perfect submissive. Perhaps it was true. She had never been truly tested. The dominants she had been with cared less about her submission than in how they might bury their cocks in her. Though he had eventually succumbed to her charms, Gallant had taken her only after she had forced the situation—and in a manner she still felt guilty over.

She would make amends for her bad behavior. He would see a better side of her. He would see that she could be the perfect submissive for him.

Chapter Four

Y ou are free tonight, Master Gallant?"
Hazel eyes peered at him from above a
fluttering fan. Though Charles had not been at the
Red Chrysanthemum for long since his return from the
Orient, he had come to know many of the members,
especially those who quartered at the inn. Miss Sophia was
perhaps the prettiest of those.

They stood nearly where he and Miss Terrell had stood
five nights before when the young blackamoor had first
blocked his path, much as Miss Sophia now did, and
attempted to seduce him. He remembered all too clearly
how Miss Terrell's tongue had emerged between thick lips
to lick at one of the buttons of his waistcoat.

"I saw Lord Wendlesson escort his wife into a room
and close the door behind them," Miss Sophia explained,
lowering her fan to reveal demure lips rouged with a shiny
rose tint. She fluttered the fan against her bosom, drawing
attention to the two orbs swelling above the décolletage.
They appeared incongruously large for her slender frame.

She lowered her lashes as well as her voice. "I, too, am
not otherwise occupied."

"Alas, my time is engaged," he replied, feeling the
bundle tucked beneath an arm.

"Oh? And who is the fortunate skirt?"

"It is not for the purpose you think, but I would be

much obliged if you knew where Miss Terrell might be?"

A practiced coquette would have hid her frown behind the fan, but Miss Sophia did nothing to hide her visible displeasure.

"I know she occupies a new room, with Miss Sarah, I believe," Miss Sophia replied, unable to keep the bitterness from her tone.

Not wanting others to think that there was anything more than an innocent involvement between him and Miss Terrell, he said, "Would you mind informing her that I await her in the dining hall?"

Miss Sophia drew in a sharp breath but replied, "If it pleases you, Master Gallant. I would do *anything* you wished."

She spoke the last statement, pregnant with promise, behind her fan. In his society beyond the Red Chrysanthemum, he was accustomed to how her sex employed the fan, teasing *his* sex, dancing in front and behind the delicate instrument like a prancing mouse might do to entice a mate. If Miss Sophia had been born into the *ton*, she could have taken her place among the most seasoned coquettes at Almack's.

But he preferred women without artifice. Miss Greta Barlow, with her humble breeding, was more to his liking. Or Miss Terrell, who hid nothing and could assume the role of predator better than any rakehell.

He bowed his appreciation to Miss Sophia and stood aside to allow her passage. She gave him one last smile before ascending the stairs. He turned and headed to the parlor to await Miss Terrell.

Unlike Miss Sophia, Miss Terrell would not have relented so easily. He shook his head, remembering how she had pressed her suit till he had to pick her up and set her aside. Undeterred, she had trapped him in a room, refusing to hand over the key. He had given her a sound spanking for her mischief. Fortunately, he had found the key easily, but that spanking had set in motion his undoing.

No derriere was as supple as hers. The blood had not coursed to his cock when his hand connected with that fine flesh, it had *careened*, lust barreling into his body swifter than any horse at Ascot. When she had had him bound to the chair—the audacious, wicked minx—completely at her mercy, he had done his best to resist her charms, calling upon every ounce of his anger for her depraved deed. He was still astounded that she had dared force herself upon him in such fashion. He suspected she had enlisted the aid of Jones, the blackamoor employed to keep order at the inn, to hold him down. They had both violated protocol in doing what they did and should be banned from the Red Chrysanthemum.

But Charles had not the heart to see either of them thrown into the streets. When he had approached Jones, the man had seemed genuinely confounded that anything could be amiss.

"Did it not please you, sir?" Jones had asked. "I thought—it seem some dominant sorts take that other place from time to time. And some—nay, many—be partial to having themselves forced upon."

"What exactly did Miss Terrell say to you?" Charles had asked.

The large man rubbed the back of his neck and looked down at his shuffling feet. "I don't recollect much."

Charles had not pressed the matter. He believed that Jones did not attend Miss Terrell's words as much as he had her other attributes.

"It came as a surprise to me," Charles had said.

Here Jones's eyes had widened with concern. "I hope—forgive me, sir—"

"You need not worry. Miss Terrell merely wanted my undivided attention, which I had refused to grant her. She and I have resolved the matter in need of addressing. But I am concerned if you should surprise a member who may be less agreeable to such tactics. Lest you have been instructed by Joan, I would err on the side of caution."

"Yes, sir, thank you, sir."

Clearly there needed to be a protocol in place. He would take the matter up with Joan when he had considered what he would recommend and what he might say if she questioned what had prompted him to begin with?

In the modest dining hall, Charles took a seat at a small table and placed the package upon it. Thinking of the contents inside reminded him of his own transgression last night. He had *heard* but not *listened* to her pleas to keep her shirt. Overcome with anger and a need to assert his dominance, he had ripped the garment.

In his travels in the Orient, he had seen maimed body parts, old blind women, and children thin as reeds with the bones of their rib cages showing from want of flesh and food. But he had seen nothing before like Miss Terrell's scarred and mutilated back. Every other part of her was perfectly beautiful. He could not recall when he had last felt such sickness in his stomach upon seeing the ghastly terrain of her back. No woman deserved to be beaten in such fashion.

That hers was the greater offense last night did not mitigate his fault nor dampen his anguish. He half wanted to meet this overseer who had the cruelty to administer a brutal flogging to a young woman. What Charles might do to the man would likely land him in Newgate.

Hearing footsteps approach, he looked up and was startled at the vision before him.

He was accustomed to seeing Miss Terrell in attire that reminded him of country servants and milkmaids. But tonight she stood before him in an appropriate gown. She had worn one yester evening, but in the darkness of night, he had not taken much note of its appearance. Tonight, she had clearly attempted more grooming, for her hair was pulled from her countenance and wrapped neatly atop her head, with only a ringlet gracing either side of her face with as much effect as the prettiest of earrings. Her eyes sparkled. As did her smile. That she was plainly pleased to see him warmed his heart.

He rose quickly to his feet and made a small bow. "Miss Terrell."

"Master Gallant," she responded in a manner he might have deemed uncharacteristically shy, but for the small grin tugging at one corner of her lips.

As with Miss Sophia, she had applied rouge that made her lips glisten. Miss Terrell had the softest, fullest lips he had ever kissed. He remembered well how supple they had felt beneath his own.

He pulled out a chair for her. She took it gracefully, and he was reminded that she had once been a courtesan to gentlemen. How many, he knew not, and would not inquire. Leastways, not at the moment. Dressed in proper clothing, her thick, curly hair tamed into order, she looked as old as twenty. He had worried that she might not be as old as she had stated.

"You are not with the viscount and Miss Katherine this evening," she said.

"Wendlesson has decided to assume the instruction of

his wife," he replied, taking his seat opposite her.

Her eyes lit up. "How grand!"

Her fervor surprised him.

"That is, it must please Miss Katherine," she said. "Not that she would not have excelled under your instruction, but I think her very much in love with her husband."

"I require no consolation," he assured her. "From the beginning, I had hoped Wendlesson would take responsibility for instructing his own wife."

He half expected her to remark that he would now have more time for *her*, but she said only, "I am happy for Miss Katherine."

He believed her but could not resist remarking, "You do not mourn the loss of Lord Wendlesson's company?"

She started, and he immediately regretted his words. The quickness with which jealousy had reared its head surprised him. Though he had spoken without acrimony, she flushed and her thick lashes fluttered. He recalled when he had once, in so many words, called her a whore. Though she had seemed taken aback, she had rebounded swiftly, almost defying him to resist her all the same.

She could not dispute the label of a whore for she was a woman who traded her favors for money. And quite the sum at that. With Sir Arthur as her patron, she was perhaps the largest single generator of income for the Red Chrysanthemum. Charles wondered what percentage of Sir Arthur's coin Joan kept for herself.

"I am satisfied if his lordship does not mourn the loss of *my* company," Terrell replied.

Observing her lifted chin, he wondered if the woman allowed anything to weigh upon her. He knew not why he had brought up the matter of Lord Wendlesson. He ought to have known she would not provide a response that would assuage him. What had he hoped to hear from her? That she regretted lifting her skirts to the viscount? That she had no interest in Lord Wendlesson beyond his purse strings?

"I hope that to be the case, for Miss Katherine's sake," he said.

She looked down. "Yes, well, perhaps I ought— perhaps I was hasty in…"

To his surprise, she sounded *regretful*.

"They might not have come together without your contribution," he comforted. "If we had not succeeded, who knows what path Wendlesson might have pursued next. They have more hope now than they did before."

Her countenance brightened. "Yes! We have done well with their instruction. I should say we make a fine team, Master Gallant."

He realized he had used the word "we" first. The thought of working in tandem once more with Miss Terrell piqued his curiosity, but such a prospect would only bode ill for them both. He wondered if he might not think differently, were Sir Arthur absent from the equation.

"Nevertheless," Charles said, "you should keep your distance from Wendlesson, that Miss Katherine might have all his attention."

"I have no intention of seducing his lordship."

It is you I wish to seduce, her eyes said. The blood coursed to his groin.

"And I think his interest in me limited," she continued. "I do not think he favors dark flesh. Mine merely happened to be the only cunnie present at the time he needed relief."

Recalling his exchange with Wendlesson from a few nights before, when both men had disavowed any partiality for a blackamoor, and how Miss Terrell might have overheard them, Charles said, before thinking of the consequences, "If he saw how pretty you look at the moment, he would reconsider his preferences."

He had not meant to offer her any encouragement, but seeing how pleased she appeared, he decided not to care. He pushed the package over to her. "This is for you."

She cocked her head to one side. "Why do I suspect it might be a shirt?"

He smiled. "Because it is one." He looked around and saw that they were not alone in the dining hall. "And as I have spoiled the mystery, I think it best you open the package in the privacy of your chambers. It would attract too much curiosity otherwise."

She pushed the package across the table to him. "Thank you, but I pray you keep it for yourself. I asked for your time, not a new shirt."

He slid the package back. "It would not fit me. My tailor thinks I had it sewn for a nephew, though I haven't any nephews. I ruined yours. It is only fitting I replace it."

She intended to push the package back, but he had kept his hand upon it. She pursed her supple lips. "If it was ruined, it was my doing. I don't…I don't deserve to have it replaced."

"A shirt is easier to give than my time, yet you have no qualms asking for the latter."

Her lips fell into a frown. Brow furrowed, she looked down once more. It was a different side of her that he was seeing tonight. The panther lacked the self-assured bravado he was accustomed to, but the audacious huntress was not gone for long.

"I suppose you think me more ridden with greed than guilt," she said. "Well, where you are concerned, Master

Gallant—and you may be as flattered as you please—I will be greedy. I have made it plain that I want you, though I would settle for one night. If you would take me as your submissive for one night, I would be happy."

Her words made his cods boil, drawing most of his attention to the areas below his waist. Lowering his voice, he managed to say, "Have we not already indulged ourselves and agreed to its imprudence?"

She shook her head. "I want it all, Master Gallant. My complete submission for your complete dominance."

The blood pounded between his legs, his cock stretching at thoughts he had vowed not to entertain. But then, he should never have agreed to grant her his time. He had knowingly made his own life difficult.

"Till then, you may keep your shirt." She shoved it past his hand.

He looked from the package to her and narrowed his eyes. "Are you refusing me, Miss Terrell?"

Her lower lip fell. His gaze went there immediately. He could not have known that when he had invited her participation onto the stage where he was disciplining Greta—Mistress Scarlet, as the members knew her—that she would be testing his forbearance afterward. He remembered well how those soft, full lips had felt beneath his own, and he was inclined to take them once more. But while he had accepted that Greta would not return to London or that she would not receive him even if she did, he was not prepared for another to take her place. His cock felt otherwise, but Charles was determined that sense should prevail over primitive carnal sensibilities.

"Do behave," he said sternly, "and accept the shirt."

He did not push the package back to her but waited patiently to see what she would do. She was not inclined to docility and obedience. He had told her as much. It was why she would not make a good submissive, despite her boasts to the contrary. She had claimed she could be a perfect submissive, but he did not believe her for a minute. Miss Greta had done the same and had not made good her avowal.

Miss Terrell reached across the table and pulled the package to her. "Thank you, Master Gallant."

"You are more than welcome. I pray you wear it in good health."

A muscle along his jaw rippled as he considered what her shirt had concealed before he had torn it asunder, not knowing the garment hid her disfigured back. No one should have to suffer the lashes she had endured.

Though he dreaded the answer, he had to ask, "What else did the overseer, this Mr. Tremayne, do to you?"

She said nothing at first. When she spoke, it was devoid of the anguish and bitterness he would have expected.

"It was after my lashing that I was determined to make it into the Great House at any cost. And I was fortunate I was able to do so."

"It is impressive that you can manage gratitude amidst these tribulations," he said.

"Those who have not the advantage of beauty or skill are condemned to the fields or the boiling houses. Once, when I had displeased the mistress, she sent me back to the fields, but my master missed my company enough to recall me back to the Great House."

He shifted in his seat at what part of her "company" the man must have missed most. "How many slaves were there?"

"A hundred or so, not including the children."

"Children? How many children were there?"

"A mere dozen. Most of the women, like myself, are incapable of conceiving." Her voice wavered slightly, but she continued once more in her detached tone, "Children are not encouraged. Like the old, they are considered a drain upon the plantation. They are of no use until they are four or five years of age. It is more…economical, I believe, to purchase a new slave off the ships than raise a slave from birth. Have I used the appropriate word? Economical?"

"Yes, you have used 'economical' correctly. How is it you have mastered speech so well? You have not long been in gentle society."

"While it was not necessary to speak well in Barbados, I saw that things were different here. If I wanted the attention of gentlemen, if I wanted better treatment, then I needed to sound more…refined. I studied, I imitated, I listened for hours on end, often to the most inane conversations. I asked questions of words I did not understand. Sir Fairchild was quite tolerant of it all. I merely had to hold out the right enticement."

A corner of her lips quirked in a smile. He could not return it. He knew too well what sort of enticement she meant. Once more, the sensation of jealousy surprised him.

"Learning to read was much harder," she said. "Mr. Terrell, before he became ill, attempted to instruct me. No one else has had the patience or inclination. I once traded my favors to a footman to have him teach me, but he soon became demanding and tiresome. He wanted my favors first, then was often too fatigued to learn me much."

"You need not always use your body as currency."

She cocked a brow. "What else do I have? Offering my body costs me nothing."

He pressed his lips into a firm line. "Well, I will accept no payment in return to learn you what I can."

"*You*, I should like to repay," she murmured.

"Let us have the book, Miss Terrell," he responded before he was pulled too deeply into the brightness of her eyes.

She handed him *Fanny Hill*. He adjusted himself beneath the table before drawing his chair next to hers. He knew not how to instruct a person on letters and reading. For tonight, he would simply read. She might come to know some words by sight.

"*Memoirs of a Woman of Pleasure*," he said, drawing his finger beneath each word as he read. He opened the book. "'Letter the first. I sit down to give you an undeniable proof of my considering your desires as indispensable orders. Ungracious then as the task may be, I shall recall to view those scandalous stages of my life, out of which I emerged, at length, to the enjoyment of every blessing in the power of love, health and fortune to bestow; whilst yet in the flower of youth, and not too late to employ the leisure afforded me by great ease and affluence, to cultivate an understanding, naturally not a despicable one, and which had, even amidst the whirl of loose pleasures I had been tossed in, exerted more observation on the characters and manners of the world than what is common to those of my unhappy profession, who, looking on all thought or reflection as their capital enemy, keep it at as great a distance as they can, or destroy it without mercy.'"

She listened in rapt attention, staring at the words as if she could glean their secrets. He stole a glance at her profile, at thick black lashes, high but subtle cheekbones, a perfectly unblemished complexion, and lips so full they appeared always to be pouting.

"'Hating, as I mortally do, all long unnecessary prefaces, I shall give you good quarter in this, and use no farther apology, than to prepare you for seeing the loose part of my life, written with the same liberty that I led it.

"'Truth! stark, naked truth, is the word; and I will not so much as take the pains to bestow the strip of a gauze wrapper on it, but paint situations such as they actually rose to me in nature, careless of violating those laws of decency that were never made for such unreserved intimacies as ours; and you have too much sense, too much knowledge of the originals, to sniff prudishly and out of character at the pictures of them. The greatest men, those of the first and most leading taste, will not scruple adorning their private closets with nudities, though, in compliance with vulgar prejudices, they may not think them decent decorations of the staircase, or salon.'"

"'Tis true!" Miss Terrell remarked. "Though, in the case of Sir Fairchild, it was his wife who would not permit paintings of this nature, but the walls of the apartment he kept for me were adorned with them."

A member of White's, Charles knew of Sir Fairchild from the club, and what little he had seen of the man did not suggest him to be one whom Charles would wish greater acquaintance with.

"Was Sir Fairchild kind to you?" he asked Terrell.

She considered his question. "He provided me lodging, clothing and pin money."

"But was he kind to you?"

She looked him in the eyes, and he was struck by how she would unabashedly meet his gaze. "Kind enough. I would have stayed with him if I could. He was far better than the others, all except Mr. Terrell, that is."

Charles looked at the book he held. No good

information could come of his inquiries, but he could not resist wanting to know more of Miss Terrell and her past.

"That does not necessarily speak well of Sir Fairchild," he said grimly.

She shrugged. "He never struck me."

"And that is the criterion by which you deem a man 'kind enough'?"

She raised a brow. "Compared to my life in Barbados, my circumstances here in England are quite agreeable. Sir Fairchild, at the least, was happy when drunk. There are men who become angry when intoxicated. I was briefly mistress to an Italian count who struck me with a fire poker and threw chamber pots at my head."

His jaw tightened.

"The worst Sir Fairchild would do was make me crawl about the floor snorting and grunting like a sow might do."

"He did *what?*"

"Sir Fairchild was rather portly. I think he was not fond of his corpulence, and it amused him to think he was fucking swine. Also, he made me cheat at cards when we played whist."

Charles hoped he would not cross paths with Sir Fairchild a time too soon or he would be tempted to make a comment—or sound—that would hardly pass for courteous.

"What of Sir Arthur? How does he treat you?"

"Generously."

"Beyond the generosity of his purse, how does he treat you? Is he, too, 'kind enough'?"

"I am only concerned with his coin. But if you must know, he has not struck me."

He was relieved to hear it. He had meant to inquire

into Sir Arthur's past, for he had heard vague references to the man's temper.

But as soon as she had made her statement, she hesitated. It was brief, lasting but a second.

"Why do you pause?" he asked.

"Because I was done speaking," she responded, a little too quickly.

"Has Sir Arthur lifted a hand to you?"

"He has not struck me," she insisted.

"Do you think he could?"

"Any man is capable of violence."

"If he were to harm you or insist upon anything against your wishes, you have only to speak to Madame. All members, no matter how rich their purse, must abide by the rules. Have you established a safety word with Sir Arthur?"

"Sir Arthur is not your concern. And neither am I."

His nostrils flared. If she were his submissive... But she was not.

"Will you not read some more, Master Gallant?"

Reluctantly, even though dwelling on Sir Arthur brought him no pleasure, Charles continued reading the brief background of Miss Fanny Hill, how she had lost her parents at the tender age of fifteen, and how she found her way to London.

"Poor Fanny," Miss Terrell said after the heroine had been deserted by a woman she had deemed a friend and protectress. "I was fortunate that my acquaintance with London was facilitated by Mr. Terrell."

He looked at her with some admiration. "That you could pity this fictional character after all that you have suffered is rather remarkable."

"My circumstances provide me empathy for those who

suffer. I know what 'tis like to be buffeted by the whims of fate, to have no control over your destiny."

"Yet you persist as if you could rule your providence. A lesser man would have had his spirit cowed, broken, by what you have been through. But you are hardly meek or weakened. I find it hard to reconcile your experiences with your present demeanor."

"You think I have lied to you?"

"No. That is not what I meant."

"Are you unfamiliar with the accounts of slave life?"

"I have read a little of what Mr. Thomas Clarkson has written."

"Did you support Sir Wilberforce's efforts to abolish the slave trade?"

"I was in the Orient at the time Parliament took up the matter, but I was glad to hear of its passage. If I should be fortunate to be a burgess, I should seek legislation to curb the cruelty of overseers and slave owners. The men who inflicted the atrocities you described must be brought to justice and punished for their unspeakable acts."

"It would be easier to abolish the institution of slavery than to attempt to try and sentence individual men."

"Slavery does not exist in the British Isles."

"But it exists in her colonies."

He hesitated. "Much of the economy is dependent upon slavery."

"Do you condone slavery?"

"I do not."

"They why defend it?"

"I was hardly defending it. But it took no small effort to abolish the slave trade. I doubt Parliament is ready to take further action on the matter."

Her brow furrowed in disappointment, and he could

not help but be affected by it.

"The only bondage I truly support is the kind that takes place within these walls," he said.

Her frown turned into a smile. "I particularly like the sort of bondage you impose, Master Gallant."

That was more of what he had expected from her. Once more, he felt the heat stir in his groin. He was fortunate that they had not yet come upon the more salacious passages in *Fanny Hill*.

He remembered the first time he had read from the novel to Miss Terrell. He had bound her to the bedposts. She could not move her limbs. She could not touch herself. He had then chosen a most wanton episode to read. It had been no easy task to watch how his reading had aroused her to distraction, how she could do nothing to address that divine agitation in her loins, without wanting to do something to her. But she had required a disciplining for her waywardness during a lesson with the viscountess. A lesson she had insinuated herself into.

In the end, Miss Terrell's participation had turned out for the best for Miss Katherine, and he told himself that was what mattered, though he would have thought himself a man who did not use the end to justify the means. But Miss Terrell had a way of turning things on their heads, testing him and causing him to question himself. It was unsettling, frightening, and titillating all at once.

He expected her to follow her statement with an act, such as putting her hand upon his thigh, intended to ignite his ardor. She required no grand movements, for his cock responded to the smallest of her endeavors. Her mere nearness warmed his body more effectively than a vibrant hearth.

Needing a distraction, he returned to the book. He read

further of how Fanny came to find lodging with Mrs. Brown, innocently believing she had been hired to look after her mistress' linen. Fanny was then given into the care of Phoebe.

"'It was here agreed that I should keep myself up and out of sight for a few days, till such clothes could be procured for me as were fit for the character I was to appear in, of my mistress' companion, observing withal, that on the first impressions of my figure much might depend; and, as they rightly judged, the prospect of exchanging my country clothes for London finery, made the clause of confinement digest perfectly well with me. But the truth was, Mrs. Brown did not care that I should be seen or talked to by any, either of her customers, or her Does (as they called the girls provided for them), till she secured a good market for my maidenhead, which I had at least all the appearances of having brought into her Ladyship's service.'"

He knew what came next. They had read aloud with Miss Katherine of Fanny's first licentious experience at the hands of her tutoress. The scene of Miss Terrell caressing Miss Katherine, the pretty blackamoor pleasuring the naive innocent, flashed through his mind. As did many other memories. Miss Terrell's lovely arse bent over the back of a chair. Their congress in the dark alley. Her mouth encapsulating his cock whilst he was bound to a chair.

The last one drew mixed emotions still. He had forgiven her the transgression, but a part of him still felt he had a score to settle with her. His helplessness at her hands had both enraged and titillated. Her boldness unsettled him and made him feel less assured. The Master in him wanted to reclaim control—establish control, rather, for he wondered that he ever had hegemony when it came to

Miss Terrell.

Scanning the next few paragraphs and seeing the words "embraced and kissed with great eagerness," "wandered over my whole body," and "lambent fire," he wished he had suggested they read from a different book. A more mundane book. Even *Tom Jones* would prove easier than plodding through the very lustful, very descriptive writings of Mr. Cleland.

Charles closed the book. "Let us continue another night."

She started, then frowned. "But we have not come across the most exciting parts."

"I have a great many appointments tomorrow."

He spoke truthfully, but it was not the reason he wished to call an end to the evening with her.

Her mouth formed a pout. How he would have liked nothing more than to have those supple lips wrapped about his cock once more!

"As you wish, Master Gallant," she said at last, perhaps appeased at the prospect of having his company for another night. "Thank you for reading to me."

He drew his chair back to the other side of the table. "You're most welcome."

"Will you read to me tomorrow?"

As he had expected to be instructing Miss Katherine the following night, he had the time, but a day's absence from Miss Terrell might calm the lust she always seemed to ignite.

"What of Sir Arthur?" he asked as he adjusted the crotch of his pants beneath the table.

"Sir Arthur comes early in the evening, but I do not expect him at all tomorrow. He is off to Dressex for hunting and will be gone ten days, perhaps more."

Charles did not know how to receive such information. A part of him was undeniably delighted. He did not particularly like Sir Arthur and tolerated the man out of respect for his own employer, Sir Canning, and the fact that Sir Arthur, who owned nearly half of Porter's Hill, could hand the election to Charles on a gilded platter.

"Sir Arthur will expect your attentions upon his return, no doubt," he said.

"Yes, but would you not say his absence presents a nice opportunity?"

He knew exactly what she intended with the occasion, and it was tempting. So very tempting.

"I promise to read more," he said, "and will consider the possibility of doing so tomorrow evening."

"You are not otherwise engaged, for you are now relieved of your instruction to Miss Katherine. Why will it not be tomorrow?"

Her eyes looked brightly at him, pleading, reminding him of a child who had the prospect of receiving a new pony the next day.

"There are days my campaigning drains me. A respite from the Red Chrysanthemum might improve my weariness."

"You have never appeared weary."

Because she had always managed to rouse him, for good and bad, no matter what his mood.

"Miss Terrell, a good submissive does not quarrel with her Master."

Her eyes lit up, and she sat upright. "Are you my Master?"

"I am merely advising you as to proper submissive behavior. Your actions thus far do not reflect your prior assertions of being a perfect submissive."

Chastened, she sank back into the chair. She lowered her lashes. "Yes, Master."

The words made his blood percolate. A quick departure was in his best interest. "Good night, Miss Terrell."

"Good night, Master Gallant. And...thank you."

It was a heartfelt appreciation. He could see the sincerity in the luminescence of her eyes. She had very striking eyes. The pupils were so dark, the whites so white. The crease of her eyelids made the eyes appear twice as large.

Feeling as if he could lose himself in their depths, he made her a bow and took his leave before he was enticed to stay.

As he waited for his hat and gloves in the foyer, he wondered what it would be like to have Miss Terrell as a submissive. Surely it could not end more disastrously than his time with Miss Greta. With Sir Arthur gone, he could grant Miss Terrell her one night. Or three. He would not delude himself into thinking that one would be enough. He had tasted of her quim more than once, and his appetite was hardly satiated. He could, at his own hand, relieve the tension churning in his loins, but why should he deny himself a far superior way to spend?

Stepping out of the inn to his horse, he welcomed the cooler night air. Of all the seasons, he had always liked autumn most. The weather suited him. And the colder temperatures would bring a greater appreciation for ale among the voters. Though he would need more than ale to sway a voter, if what Mr. Warren had claimed was true. The returning officer had told Charles that Mr. Laurel, the one Whig candidate in the race, was offering twenty shillings per vote.

Charles considered the importance of Sir Arthur once

more. The MP was inclined to support him, provided he do nothing to upset the man. But Charles was loath to be in the man's pocket. The two differed greatly in their approaches to China. Sir Arthur wanted to force trade with the aid of cannons. And they were likely to disagree over India as well. Charles did not approve of the opium being smuggled into China by the East India Company, which Sir Arthur oversaw as a member of the Board.

He was not convinced that Sir Arthur was the only means of winning the election. But he would need the support of the Brentwoods to win without Sir Arthur. Mr. and Mrs. Brentwood had helped elect many a burgess for Porter's Hill. Alas, the senior Gallant had not been one of them, but between Sir Arthur's support, ready for the taking, and Lord Wendlesson's letter of introduction, Charles had opportunities his father never had.

Upon arriving at his townhouse, however, Charles realized he did not have Lord Wendlesson's letter with him. He searched his coat pockets nonetheless before he was convinced of its whereabouts. He had held the letter in conjunction with the wrapped shirt prior to presenting it to Miss Terrell.

She was now in possession of the letter.

Chapter Five

Terrell examined the letter. She recognized the Wendlesson seal upon the back. It was addressed to a Mr. and Mrs. Brentwood. She thought of returning the letter to Wendlesson, but the letter must have been in Gallant's possession, for it had lain beneath the package containing the shirt he had gifted her. What if the letter somehow belonged to Master Gallant? Her pulse quickened.

Tucking the letter into the strings of the package, she left the dining hall and bumped into Sophia. The comely young woman arched a delicate brow.

"You and Master Gallant looked quite *intimate*. Do you not have your hands full with Sir Arthur?" she inquired. "I know if I had Sir Arthur for a patron, I should not be such a greedy wench as to try to ensnare Master Gallant as well."

"But I *am* such a greedy wench." Terrell could not resist.

Disgruntled, Sophia said nothing at first. Her gaze then took in the package Terrell held. "I saw Master Gallant in possession of just such a bundle. I assume you did not steal it from him, though your kind is given to thievery and felony."

Sophia spoke with the intent to vex. Therefore, Terrell prevailed if she refused to allow the flaxen-haired beauty to irk her, but try as she might, she could not eschew her irritation.

"Indeed, I've not your talent for stealing," Terrell retorted, alluding to the time Sophia had been caught pilfering a guinea from a patron's purse.

Sophia's eyes flared in anger. Terrell brushed by the woman before their quarrel escalated.

A fortnight ago, Terrell had wanted nothing more than to leave the Red Chrysanthemum for good. Before Sir Arthur, Madame had paired her with a visiting patron who had insisted she rub his foul-smelling corn-covered feet before they proceeded with anything. There had been an abominable odor about his whole body. If she had not died from being smothered beneath his large frame, she'd thought she might suffocate from his stench. She had vowed that as soon as could land a patron to whom she might become a mistress, she would be free of the Red Chrysanthemum. She could return to her previous glory as a courtesan to men of wealth and influence. Only this time, she had learned her lesson. She would have a supply of money to draw from should her paramour ever tire of her and cast her off penniless, as Sir Fairchild had done. She would not have to resort to places like the Red Chrysanthemum.

The advent of Master Gallant had changed all that. She still needed to attach herself to a man with funds, a man such as Sir Arthur, but suddenly, she was in less of a hurry to depart the Red Chrysanthemum. There had been numerous times tonight when she had wanted to touch Gallant. His nearness set her senses on fire, even the olfactory ones. He had a delicious aroma about him, of cleanliness and masculinity. Everything about him was delicious. His elegant dress, his deportment, his voice, his hands—hands possessed of such control they could be as gentle as that of a woman's, yet land such powerful blows upon the rump.

Terrell shivered. She had known within minutes of observing him that she wanted him, that he was more skilled than any other Master here. The rope bondage he had displayed with Mistress Scarlet had awed everyone. Terrell had been more than thrilled when he had first wrapped the ropes about her own limbs, though it had not ended as she had wished. He had bound her wrists and stretched them to the rafters, leaving her in the position for a good half hour before Tippy, the dressing maid, came upon her. Though she had been a little infuriated at him, the memory of it now warmed her loins. It seemed Master Gallant could do nothing that did not arouse her.

In her room, she found Sarah sitting at the bed knitting stockings for George, who slept beside her, snoring softly.

"How fared your evening with Master Gallant?" Sarah asked.

Terrell set the parcel down upon the bed. "We were both of us well behaved."

"How disappointing."

Terrell smiled. "Yes, but I enjoyed his company nonetheless."

It occurred to her then that if she could have Master Gallant in no other way, she would be content to have him read to her than to have none of his company.

Sarah raised her brows. "Are you certain you are in no danger of succumbing to 'that sort of infatuation'?"

Terrell could make no reply. Love was not something she had ever aspired to, especially with his kind. While she wanted Gallant in her bed, her path out of the Red Chrysanthemum was Sir Arthur. If he would take her for a mistress and provide her lodging, clothing and pin money, she will have obtained the best situation a person of her background could attain.

"I should be a little in love with Master Gallant, I think," Sarah said. "A man with his disposition would have suited me much better than Sir Rowen. What is that parcel you have?"

"A shirt, I believe."

"A shirt?"

"To replace my old one."

"Is it from Master Gallant?"

Terrell hesitated, still uneasy over the events that had resulted in her torn shirt. She did not begrudge Master Gallant for ripping her garment and exposing her deformity. He had been infuriated over her actions. The look of shock, then revulsion, upon his handsome countenance had made her ill to the core. But she had done worse. She had held him against his will. And yet he had forgiven her. Perhaps it was pity that had moved him to such ready forgiveness. She had felt rather undeserving of his clemency.

He had not only forgiven her, he had taken her, had thrust into her as if he desired her, despite her ugliness. He desired her still. She had sensed it even as he sat across the table from her. She was certain if she had placed her hand between his thighs, his cock would have hardened, if it had not already. He had ended the reading rather abruptly.

"Yes," Terrell answered as she untied the strings of the parcel.

"You received a shirt from Master Gallant?"

Terrell made no response and opened the wrapping. By look alone, she could discern that the new shirt was of much finer quality than that which it replaced. She fingered the softness of the linen and admired the bright white coloring. She had not owned clothing of such whiteness since her days as a courtesan.

"That is a fine garment," Sarah remarked.

Wanting to feel it about her, Terrell began removing the pins in her gown. Sarah put down her knitting and sat behind her to assist.

"What became of your old one?" Sarah asked.

"It was thin and worn and wanted replacing."

"How kind of Master Gallant to gift you a new one. He must be a little partial to you."

She would have liked to believe that the case, but the words he had spoken to Lord Wendlesson still echoed in her ears.

"I have no interest in Miss Terrell," he had said to the viscount, neither of the men realizing she stood at the threshold of the room they occupied. "Her qualities do not compel me as much as they do you. If I had any interest in taking a submissive here at the Red Chrysanthemum, I assure you, it would not be Miss Terrell, even were she the last woman remaining."

If I had any interest in taking a submissive here at the Red Chrysanthemum, I assure you, it would not be Miss Terrell, even were she the last woman remaining.

The words still cut her more than she would have liked. His statements could not have been as absolute as presented. He had, of his own volition, claimed her twice. While she had found every part of those encounters exhilarating, she wanted more. She wanted his complete dominance.

"I would he were more partial," Terrell said as she slid off her gown.

"What of Sir Arthur? I hardly think him the sort of man who would tolerate your association with a rival."

Terrell remembered Sarah's account of Sir Arthur and his wife. She herself had seen sparks of his temper, and it had sent chills through her.

"Sir Arthur is gone for more than a sennight. I should be satisfied with a single night with Master Gallant."

"Then you have more than enough time to seduce him."

"Perhaps."

Terrell had never before come across a man of whom she was so uncertain. The natural carnal urges in him responded to her, but he had more forbearance than any man she knew. Since finding her freedom in England, she had never before given of herself to a man gratis. And still he declined her.

"I think he hopes for the return of Mistress Scarlet," Terrell said.

"I did not think any man could command the submission of Mistress Scarlet. I wonder that he took such an interest in her? I do not mean to speak unkindly, but she struck me as quite aloof and contemptuous of women who filled the submissive role."

"Perhaps he was attracted by the challenge. He did succeed where all others had failed." She knit her brows in thought. "Perhaps my error was in throwing myself at him and making myself too available."

"The most accomplished coquettes do often feign disinterest to draw the other sex. Desperation seems to amplify desire."

"I have seen such behavior in our sex, though it is hardly necessary or expected here."

Sarah had untied the stays. Terrell quickly shed her undergarments and pulled the new shirt overhead. She sighed as the softness of the fabric caressed her skin. The garment had loose, billowing sleeves but fit closely about the bosom, for it was plainly not cut for the shape of a woman.

"Is this, too, from Master Gallant?" asked Sarah, holding the letter. "Oh, it is addressed to a Mr. And Mrs. Brentwood."

Terrell received the letter from Sarah. "I think it must have been in Master Gallant's possession, or how would I have ended up with it? The seal upon the back is that of Lord Wendlesson."

"I believe he bears some relation to the Brentwoods, if they are whom I am thinking of. I believe the Brentwoods reside in Porter's Hill. Why would Master Gallant give you such a letter?"

"It must have been by accident. I suppose I ought return it to him if he comes tomorrow."

"You *suppose*? Why would you not?"

Terrell caught herself. She had promised to be good, to impress Master Gallant that she could be the perfect submissive. The mischievous part of her was considering how she might use the letter to her advantage.

"If the letter is intended for the Brentwoods of Porter's Hill, it might pertain to the election," Sarah added. "I know not all the other candidates, but I am certain Master Gallant would make a fine Member of Parliament."

"Yes, he would," Terrell seconded with conviction. She placed the letter beneath her pillow and began clearing away her other articles of clothing and the parcel wrapping.

Sarah went to sleep soon after, but Terrell lay awake staring into the darkness. Wearing her new shirt, she liked to think that Master Gallant held her. She embraced the garment to herself. Reaching underneath the pillow, she pulled out the letter. If it was an item of importance, Master Gallant would surely return for it on the morrow. She could not resist contemplating what she might demand from him for the return of the letter.

What a naughty wench am I, she thought to herself. Master Gallant had, on more than one occasion, said that she was too wayward to be a good submissive. His presumption riled, though she could not fault him entirely for drawing such a conclusion. Should she prove him wrong or fulfill his expectation at his peril?

She would be good, she decided. Though it was tempting to be bad. So very tempting.

Chapter Six

Sitting across the table from his mother, still as lovely as ever in his esteem, Charles watched as Mrs. Gallant reviewed a letter through a pair of spectacles perched adorably near the tip of her nose.

"I wonder if my language is too forward?" she worried. "This is my third draft, but I hesitate to take the time to write a fourth, for we have not much more than a month before Election Day."

He reached over and pushed the letter down. "My dear, I am certain the letter is as fine as it can be. You have written so many for me, you will injure your wrist if you persist in more."

"It is my duty as your mother, and I am happy to perform it, though I will not quarrel when your wife assumes part of the responsibility."

Charles thought of the women in his life. Miss Greta would not have the eloquence of Mrs. Gallant, and he doubted Miss Terrell could write more than her name, if that. But why did he contemplate Miss Terrell? She was far from an appropriate spouse for him.

"Miss Dempsey has a nice hand. I witnessed her penmanship when she wrote to thank me for a recommendation. I had passed her the name of my favorite seamstress."

"Miss Dempsey may write beautifully, but I wonder

that she will be inclined to write letters of a political purpose?"

"Why so uncharitable? You cannot know."

"She has always seemed mostly interested in looking at the fashion plates in *The Lady's Magazine*."

"That is hardly unusual for her sex. And she may take an avid interest in supporting her husband."

Charles said nothing, for he did not think Miss Dempsey to be inclined toward much self-sacrifice, but perhaps he was hasty in forming his judgment.

Mrs. Gallant looked once more to her letter. "I know the Brentwoods to be skeptical of our loyalty to blue, but they cannot overlook the fact that Sir Canning supports you, even though most consider Mr. Chester the staunchest Tory in the race."

"The Chesters have been Tories all their lives."

"Well, I suppose I ought not fret if the Brentwoods do not endorse your candidacy, for the support of Sir Arthur is sufficient. Has he said in no uncertain terms that he backs you for the burgess?"

Charles straightened and looked out the window of his parents' study. The skies were cloudy and a good wind ruffled at the trees outside. "He has not, and I would rather not rely upon his support."

"No? He owns half of Porter's Hill. It would make our efforts much easier."

"Nearly half," he corrected. "It is possible to win without Sir Arthur."

"I suppose if you had the support of the Brentwoods, it were more probable, but Sir Arthur's resources far exceed the Brentwoods'. Did you not say that Mr. Laurel is offering twenty shillings a man? Even with the support of the Brentwoods, how are we to best that?"

"Not every vote can be bought by the highest bid, but I own that it will require much more effort to succeed if I have to compete with twenty shillings."

"Is Sir Arthur so very disagreeable?"

"I have no wish to serve in Parliament as another man's puppet."

"Of course. Well, let us do our best with the Brentwoods. Alas, your father did not always see eye to eye with Mr. Brentwood. I think Mr. Brentwood took offense when your father, when he first sought the burgess, declined to join the Society for the Suppression of Vice in exchange for their support."

"If Calvin Brentwood knew of my inclinations, I doubt he would make me any offer of support."

"Fortunately, I think Mrs. Brentwood to be the one to persuade, and the proper alliances have always been her greatest consideration. I wonder if Sir Canning would write to her?"

"Sir Canning believes the support of Sir Arthur sufficient and encourages me in that direction. But if your appeal to Mrs. Brentwood does not prevail, I may have another avenue to pursue."

"Oh?"

"I know a cousin of theirs who has offered to write a letter of recommendation."

"How splendid! I hope you will take him up on his offer. If I may be candid—"

"When have I ever wished for anything less from you?"

Mrs. Gallant smiled at her youngest son. "Since your discovery of me at the Red Chrysanthemum, I have never hidden anything from you. I will speak my mind, then. If you will not depend upon Sir Arthur's support, you must secure the endorsement of the Brentwoods if you hope to win."

Charles thought of Wendlesson's letter, which, if he was not mistaken, was in the hands of Miss Terrell. He had no choice now but to return that night to the Red Chrysanthemum.

Chapter Seven

When charles arrived at the inn, the evening, as far as the Red Chrysanthemum was concerned, was still young, and most of the patrons had yet to arrive.

"The Viscount Wendlesson and his wife did come early," the doorman, Baxter, informed Charles.

"They no longer require my company," Charles replied as he removed cloak, hat and gloves.

"Ah. And I've not seen Miss Terrell about, sir."

Charles paused. He supposed he ought not be surprised his association with Miss Terrell was known. Nevertheless, he refrained from querying any of the other servants for Miss Terrell's whereabouts.

Intending to seek her out himself, he headed upstairs to where she had a room. As he came upon the hallway, he saw a little boy holding onto a small loo table serving as a candlestand, which began to lean precariously as the boy looked as if he might sit down. With quick steps, Charles scooped up the boy before the table toppled onto him.

"Oh, my!" gasped the mother, rushing over. "I turned my back but a moment. I thought the table would hold."

Holding the boy in one arm, he leaned over and picked up the table, setting it back on its feet, and replaced the candelabra.

"This handsome fellow must be yours," he said to Miss

Sarah as the little boy pawed his cheek. He gave the boy's nose a tweak and received a gurgle of laughter.

Miss Sarah beamed as she received her son back into her arms. "He is my one and only true beau."

"He has your smile."

"Does he? I always thought he looked more like his father in every way," she said, but seemed pleased as she studied her son.

"George, is it?"

"Yes, and if he could speak, I would have him thank you for saving him."

"I merely spared him a bump on the head."

George reached out to Charles.

"I think he likes you," Miss Sarah said.

"Friendly little chap," Charles responded, accepting the boy back into his arms.

"On the contrary, he is like his father and quite fastidious about the company he keeps. There is only one other here whom he willingly tolerates."

"Indeed?"

"Terrell."

Charles paused before replying, "That is fortunate, given you share quarters."

"They did take to each other almost immediately. I think Terrell would be a devoted mother if she could have a child of her own."

He knew Miss Terrell to be barren, and it had been convenient that she was. He might otherwise question the steadfastness of his caution when in her presence.

"Where might I find Miss Terrell?" he asked.

"I saw her head upstairs to the third floor."

He frowned. There was no denying the cramp of jealousy in his bosom. "Is she with a patron?"

"I think not. She was expecting, er, hoping for you. She gave me a l—"

George grabbed a fistful of his hair.

"Georgie! No!" Miss Sarah admonished.

Charles tried to free his hair from the chubby little hand. "He has a healthy grip."

"He has a fondness for hair." She pried the fingers open and took George back before he could ensnare another handful. "Your pardon, Master Gallant."

"Not at all, Miss Sarah. How are your new accommodations?"

"Much better, thanks to Terrell. She could have had the new chambers all to herself— Madame was that pleased— but she insisted that she would be lonely without me and Georgie."

"I am pleased to hear it. Is there anything else you or George might require to make your stay here more comfortable?"

"When I first came here—I had applied for the position Tippy now holds. Terrell had done the same, so we have been here an equal length of time, but she was always more assured than I. It would seem she had been here years and I but weeks, for she took me under her wing. I wonder that I could have endured this place were it not for her."

In studying Miss Sarah, he found nothing but sincerity in her countenance. She seemed to speak from the heart and not because Miss Terrell had urged her to do so.

As if reading his thoughts, Miss Sarah continued, "Even without the disadvantage of her blackness, many find her common, vulgar even."

He lowered his eyes, for he would have added wily and brazen. Admittedly, he would sooner have suspected that she acted out of self-interest than benevolence.

"But there is much good in her. She is a rough diamond, if you will."

"May I ask for what purpose you utter such kind words of her?"

"Terrell has few friends and few defenders in this world. I would that she be better treated."

"It is a testament to your qualities, madam, that you seek goodness for her. Miss Terrell is more blessed to have a true friend, such as yourself, than a dozen friends of lesser merit."

"You are too kind, Master Gallant. Terrell could not know a more superior gentleman."

Not wishing to linger for more compliments, he bowed, saying, "It was a pleasure to meet your son, Miss Sarah."

He tweaked George's nose once more, eliciting a large, open-mouthed smile with all four teeth showing. Miss Sarah curtsied before allowing him to be on his way.

As he climbed the stairs to the third floor, he considered all that Miss Sarah had said. He did not doubt that Miss Terrell had been kind to the mother and child. He had seen glimpses of Miss Terrell's protective nature in her time with Miss Katherine. If Miss Terrell had no redeeming qualities, he wondered that he would respond to her as he did. But he also found Miss Terrell far too bold for her own good and guided by self-interest. She had not insinuated herself into the instruction of Miss Katherine to assist the latter but to avail herself of an opportunity to seduce him.

Despite his mixed feelings toward her, his body desired her with an intensity that surprised him, proving that the venereal was truly separate from the rational.

Hearing a woman scream, he quickened his stride to the room at the end of the hall.

The door was half open. Inside stood the Viscount Wendlesson, naked and holding a flogger. Charles was relieved to note that it was one of the easier floggers with wide, soft tails. The viscountess, also without a shred of clothing, was tied to the tops and bottoms of the bedposts, her slender arms and legs stretched so that her body formed the letter X.

Wendlesson swung the flogger once more at her. She emitted another scream.

"Thank you, Master," she murmured afterward.

Charles noted the bright redness upon her alabaster thighs where the flogger must have struck several times. It was not a practice of his to intervene with any patron at the Red Chrysanthemum, but he was not fully confident of Wendlesson's ability to conserve where Miss Katherine was concerned.

"Do you require your safety word?" Wendlesson asked his wife, allaying some of Charles' fears.

"No, Master."

Approaching her, Wendlesson cupped a breast and kneaded the pliant flesh. He brushed his thumb over the nipple several times. Miss Katherine purred.

"Have I pleased my Master?"

"Indeed you have, my sweet."

He reached around her hips and grabbed a buttock. Charles did not need to see to know that the man's cock stood tall and hard. His own had perked at witnessing the scene.

"Then flog me once more," Miss Katherine said.

"As you wish."

Wendlesson stepped back and delivered a blow to her

thigh. Miss Katherine screamed but thanked him without hesitation. Appeased, Charles stepped away from the threshold. He had no wish to aggravate the tension collecting in his groin.

"Never would have thought you to be a Peeping Tom."

He turned to see Miss Terrell leaning against the doorframe of the adjacent room, her hands behind her back. She wore the new shirt he had given her.

And nothing else.

The hem of the shirt came down to her thighs, covering her most private part, but there was more than enough to gawk at. The sight of her bare legs instantly set his blood to boil. The limbs, hairless as that of a young child, were quite the elegant feature. His gaze traveled to her bosom. He could tell she wore no stays beneath the shirt but could see the tops of her breasts above the décolletage. His pulse pounded.

She wore her hair in a loose coiffure, allowing one's gaze to fix upon the physiognomy with less distraction. She had high, smooth cheekbones, the shape of her face a perfectly proportioned oval, and the thickest lips he had ever seen upon a woman. There was a faint blush to her cheeks and the gleam of arousal in her eyes. It pulled at his cock.

"Do we not exalt the Peeping Tom here?" he returned, his tone more husky than he intended.

She inhaled deeply in response, her bosom rising enticingly.

"Though I had less titillating reasons for bearing witness," he said with more command, hoping to temper the rising lust. "My interest in Miss Katherine's welfare does not end merely because she is no longer my student."

Miss Terrell nodded. "I, too, had looked in upon them.

I followed them after I saw them come up here."

"Have you been here a while then?"

"Till I saw that Miss Katherine was in no distress, though it was not easy to watch them, for it was beginning to have an effect upon me."

Her words had become wispy but fraught with suggestion.

"What manner of effect?" he could not resist asking, though he knew bloody well what the effect was, for he experienced the same.

"I came into this room to relieve…the tension," she said.

Drawn by her smoldering gaze, he stepped toward her. "And did you?"

"Did I?"

"Succeed in relieving your…tension?"

He now stood close enough to disrupt her breath. One more step and she would be within reach of his embrace, within reach of kissing.

"No," she answered. "I was near, but then I heard footsteps."

He closed his eyes for a moment at the thought of her throbbing, unmet desire. He could make himself mad contemplating how wet she was between the legs.

"But I am pleased that you proved to be the disruption," she said.

He took that last step. A vein in his neck throbbed. Looking down at her, he touched the ruffle of the neckline. "Was it your intent to greet me in such inappropriate attire?"

"I thought to model it for you."

Of course she did. Because she knew the effect it would have upon him. Because she intended to seduce him. Still. It mattered not that he asked for none of it, even if his cock was hard with need.

"Does it please you? Master Gallant?"

Feeling himself drawn into her vortex, he retreated a step. The blood was pounding in his ears, and he thought he could smell her arousal. She had a scent, beneath the pomade she applied far too liberally to her hair, which called to the animal in him.

"I came for my letter," he stated, not wanting to concede to her allure.

"What letter?" she returned playfully.

He was not amused. "I am in no mood for your games, Miss Terrell."

"What mood would you be in, Master Gallant?" She looked pointedly at his tented crotch.

The lust in his body provided little room for patience. "Produce the letter, Miss Terrell."

"How badly do you desire it?"

He stared at her. A muscle rippled along his jaw. His groin ached at the affront. She would play at extortion, would she? Hold his letter hostage till he submitted to her demands? What was this woman not capable of?

He most assuredly would not submit to her. He was done placating her, done tolerating her wiles. He would have the letter. On his terms.

Scooping her with one arm, he stepped into the room, slammed the door behind them, and threw her against the back of the door.

She gasped sharply. The room was not lit, but the moon cast enough light that he could see her eyes widen with surprise or alarm.

"You wish for me to dominate you, do you?" he growled, pressing his body into hers.

Eyes still wide, she seemed capable of only taking short, shallow breaths. He could feel her bosom move beneath him.

"I…uh…"

Her hesitation puzzled him. He was accustomed to seeing her as a panther, the predator. He did not expect her confusion. Why was she stupefied? This is what she wanted, what she had brought upon herself. He fisted his hand into her coiffure and yanked her hair, exposing her beautiful neck for him to kiss or bite.

"I asked you a question, Miss Terrell."

His cock was throbbing and he wondered that he could pull back now. Thankfully, she provided the necessary consent.

"Yes," she gasped. "Yes, Master. Please, Master."

Still holding her by the hair, he pressed his forehead into the door while he reigned in his ardor and refrained from simply throwing up her shirt and fucking her. Once he had collected himself, he wrenched her from the door and flipped the shirt over her head without dislodging the arms from the sleeves. He tied a knot in the garment, then stepped back to behold her nakedness. With her arms pinned back by the shirt, her bosom was thrust forward.

He expected her to smile in triumph but instead saw a little uncertainty still.

Recalling that she had disavowed the need for a safety word, he provided her one. "Your safety word is 'Fanny'."

"Yes, Master."

"Say it."

"Fanny."

Hearing a scream from the other room, they both turned their heads.

"Thank you, Master, thank you!" they heard Miss

Katherine cry.

Charles turned back to Miss Terrell. It was going to be hard enough with the stimulation Miss Terrell provided him, but he could see the sounds would have an effect upon her, too. He cupped a breast, as he had seen Wendlesson do. The orb felt firm in his palm. He slapped it to see how it would jiggle. The flesh jogged once but sprang youthfully back in place. He waited.

"Thank you, Master," she said at last.

Perhaps she was capable of being a better submissive than he thought. He gazed at the patch of curly hair at her pelvis and could not resist running his fingers through the thick hair. He tugged at it before slipping two of his fingers below. Her lashes fluttered and her breath trembled when his digits grazed her nether lips.

She was sodden.

Damnation. Tension coiled in every fiber. He wanted to thrust himself into that glorious wetness. Now. Hard. Instead, he had to call upon every ounce of forbearance. He was going to give her what she wanted. Only it would be her set-down. It would prove he was in charge. That she could not toy with him. The wayward blackamoor needed a lesson, and he would provide it.

Chapter Eight

Perhaps she ought to confess that she had had every intention of returning his letter to him, Terrell considered.

Despite the darkness of the room, she could see a determination in his eyes and a set in his jaw that she had rarely seen before. At first she had thought it was lust that compelled him, ignited by what he had witnessed of the Wendlessons, but there was something else. Anger perhaps. He thought she would not give his letter back without wresting a concession from him.

She had only meant to tease him a little. She had been on the verge of granting him his letter when he surprised her by slamming her against the door without the gentleness she would have expected from him. And then, when he had uttered those words, words that she had longed to hear since first she had witnessed his mastery, her speech had faltered.

You wish for me to dominate you, do you?

A thousand times, yes. It was what she had burned for these past several nights. She had wanted to be good. But, irony of ironies, he had made it nearly impossible for her to be good. She could still dispute his worst thoughts of her, but would he believe her? After all that she had done, why should he expect better of her? It had been foolhardy of her to even think of taunting him with the letter.

But he was giving her what she had always wanted. He

was going to dominate her. Why say anything that might disrupt him and cause him to pause?

She tugged at the shirt that imprisoned her arms, as if freeing her limbs could help her make sense of her dilemma.

Yes, she wanted his dominance, but she had wanted to earn it the way he would have wanted her to, in the manner he deserved. He was wrong to assume that she would resort to trickery.

She could set it right. She could refuse his dominance and offer to give him the letter with no further obligation.

But she could only moan as his fingers caressed her between her legs. This was fate at her most spiteful. She finally had Gallant in the way she desired but only by confirming his lowest expectations of her.

He withdrew his fingers and brushed the moisture over one of her nipples. He caught the bud between the knuckles of his fore and middle fingers and tugged. Upon its release, she grunted.

"Master," she began. She had seen the flames of lust in his eyes. It was possible he would want to dominate her no matter what she revealed of the letter.

"Pray tell you do not require your safety word already?"

His reply had her taken aback. They could hear Miss Katherine whimpering in the next room.

"Though I should not be surprised if you had overstated your abilities," he finished.

She stared at him agog. Was he testing her, mocking her, disparaging her?

"Try me," she snapped, the words leaving her before thought. "I wager I can receive more than you can serve."

His nostrils flared. "You have an aptitude for boasting, Miss Terrell. Tonight we shall prove the veracity of your assertions."

"About bloody time," she muttered.

"Pardon?"

She straightened. "Please do what you will with me, Master."

His nearness made her skin come alive, especially as she was completely naked before him.

"I suggest you not test me, Miss Terrell," he said, pinching and twisting her left nipple till she yelped.

"Yes, Master," she said between gasps.

Releasing her aching nipple, he cupped her left breast, gently cradling the orb as his gaze devoured the flesh. She liked the shape and look of her breasts and wondered what he thought of her dark brown areolas. The nipple had hardened from his earlier attention to it and protruded at him as if wanting more.

"Does my bosom meet with your satisfaction, Master?" she asked.

"It does," he acknowledged.

He rolled, kneaded and squeezed her breast, relaxing the flesh and warming it with his touch. She felt a corresponding warmth below her navel. Would he touch her there again soon?

He released her breast and gave it a hearty slap. Having been lulled into a soothing state, the smack startled her and awoke the flesh. He gave the breast several quick slaps before landing a larger blow against the side.

"Thank you, Master."

Though her breast withstood the stinging well, she knew he was but warming her for what was to come.

Sauntering over to a table, he found candle and tinderbox. After lighting a flame, he assessed the contents of the room. It was sparsely furnished. The bed was more of a low cot with but a sheet for bedclothes. Shackles dangled from each of the short posts. A shelf on the far wall housed a variety of implements that she could not discern, but it mattered not. She would welcome anything he chose.

He took a flogger and inspected it. Her breath caught. She had grown accustomed to the instrument, but she remembered her first time facing the flogger at the Red Chrysanthemum had been filled with trepidation. It had brought back painful memories from the past.

Master Gallant would not wield the flogger in a vicious way. She trusted him in a way she had never trusted anyone before. But he seemed cross with her. And he was but human, capable of succumbing to passions of the moment.

She watched him replace the flogger and select a crop. She licked her bottom lip in anticipation. It seemed she had wanted this for an eternity. Because she had not expected it to happen tonight, had expected it would take several more nights before she would see the fruits of her seduction, her anticipation was colored with the start of a small modicum of fear. What if she could not make good on her claims? She very much wanted to be the best submissive he had ever had.

Gallant returned to her and placed the crop upon the table. He held in his hands a pair of small clamps joined together by a short chain.

"I assume you know the purpose of these," he said.

"Yes, Master."

She braced herself as he affixed a clamp to her nipple. He looked to see her reaction, but she maintained a stoic countenance. He fixed the second clamp to her other nipple and stepped back to assess the result. The clamps were a little heavy, but he had placed their jaws at the base of her nipples, and she tolerated the discomfort fairly easily. He stepped back toward her and gently pulled the chain. She grunted as the clamps tugged at her nipples. He looped the chain over her bottom lip.

"Do not drop it," he commanded as she bit down upon the chain.

The shortness of the chain ensured a constant tugging of her nipples. The heat in her loins seemed to collect in that other sensitive bud. He had touched here there but once this evening. How long would she have to wait for his caress?

She wondered how she would utter her safety word while holding the chain in her mouth, but she had once boasted she would not require a safety word, so she supposed it would not matter.

He pulled a wooden chair over to where she stood. Setting it down in front of her, he cupped the back of her neck and pulled her down over the back of the chair till it nestled beneath her breasts. Leaving her bent over the chair, he went to turn the lock in the door should any of the arriving guests desire the room. Her heart skipped at the prospect that he would make use of the room for a good length of time.

"Thank you, Master, thank you!" she heard Miss Katherine cry.

Taking his time, Gallant began removing his clothes: his coat, his neckcloth, his collar. Terrell hoped he would strip to the buff. He had a beautiful body, the chiseled form of a man of sport but without the brawny muscles of a laborer. There was much to admire in his chest, his arms, his calves. And that lovely cock, of course. How divinely it had felt inside of her!

She shivered.

But he stopped undressing. Still in his shirt and pants, he picked up his neckcloth and tied one end around her hair. By securing the other end to the shirt that bound her arms, he kept her head up, which further pulled upon the clamps while gravity worked her nipples in the opposite direction. He took up the crop from the table and caressed the curve of her rump with its length before giving a sound smack to one buttock.

"Where is my gratitude?" he demanded.

"Thank you, Master!" she hurried to say.

The chain dropped from her mouth.

"Failing already, Miss Terrell?"

She glowered, for her could not see her from where he stood, but he came round to the front soon enough. Squatting down, he removed the clamps. But this time he fixed them toward the tips of her nipples. She whimpered and felt her toes curl as the clamps bit into her sensitive buds.

"Let us try again," he said, putting the chain back into her mouth.

He stood and went to stand behind her once more. The crop came down upon her other buttock.

"Dang you, Masser," she said through the chain.

He smacked her again. "I cannot fathom what you are saying."

She did her best to articulate. "Dank you, Master!"

"Better."

He delivered several more blows to her rump, some causing her to come onto her toes. She thanked him after each one, though she nearly dropped the chain after the crop had struck her for the twelfth time. Her arse stung, and the chair dug into her, but she basked in her discomfort, knowing that Master Gallant inflicted it all.

She felt something hard and smooth between her legs. It was the ivory handle of the crop sliding between her thighs. It inched upward to the lips of her cunnie, where her moisture greased its path. She moaned in delight as the edge of the handle grazed her clitoris. She would have preferred his fingers, but the sensations, in contrast to the pain elsewhere, seemed heaven-sent. The handle sawed against her cunnie till pleasure overtook the pain.

"Er-miffon who fend, Masser."

"If you are asking permission to spend and think I would grant it so readily, you are gravely mistaken,"

He withdrew the handle. She groaned at the loss. Her attention tilted back toward the pain of her burning arse and smarting nipples. The crop came down once more on her arse.

She mumbled her best thank you.

He rained the crop down upon her several more times before providing her a respite and because they heard a knocking upon the wall. It was the bed in the Wendlesson room, bumping against the wall with a constancy that left no doubt as to the rutting occurring next door. They listened for a few minutes. She could discern Lord Wendlesson's grunts and Miss Katherine's cries of delight. The expressions of their carnal engagement burned her ears, making her ache deep in her cunnie.

As if sensing her distress, Gallant slid his hand between her legs. She was soaking. He rubbed her in exquisite fashion as the sounds next door grew in volume and urgency. It was not long before she found herself on that same ascent toward ecstasy, hers fueled in part by the pain in her derriere and nipples.

Her teeth began to clatter against the chain as he

quickened his ministrations. "Huh-lease, Masser..."

Her legs trembled as she drew near the precipice. But he removed his hand, denying her the nascent release. Huffing, she knew she could do nothing. Her body in confused turmoil, she could only remain where she was, bent over the chair, her head pulled back, her nipples pulled up, as moisture dripped down her inner thigh.

Gallant as well did nothing. In the silence of their room, they listened as the viscount roared his satisfaction. The bed knocked against the wall a few times before stilling.

Filled with envy, Terrell closed her eyes. She had the feeling, for her, it was going to be a long night.

Chapter Nine

Charles listened with envy to the sound of the viscount spending. He could not discern if Miss Katherine had spent, but that he had no control over anymore. He reminded himself that he had had reservations about intervening between a married couple in the first place. Furthermore, he had his own hands full at the moment.

Turning back to Miss Terrell, so deliciously bent over the back of the wooden chair, he thought of granting himself the same satisfaction Wendleson had just achieved. She was perfectly positioned for him to plant himself behind her and ram his cock beneath that lovely rump. But he could not. Yet. He was not done providing her a set-down.

With only the light of the moon and a single candle, he could not evaluate well the markings of the crop upon her dark skin. The blush was there but muted by her blackness. She could have made use of her safety word if the crop proved too much for her, though he knew full well that he had provided her an incentive not to by placing the chain of the nipple clamps into her mouth. Deciding to err on the side of caution, however, he declined whipping her arse any further and went to stand before her. She looked up at him with large, expectant eyes. His cock twitched at the sight of the metal chain between her plump lips.

Setting aside the crop, he untied his neckcloth from her

coiffure and pulled her upright by her hair, which now leaned askew to one side of her head. She looked surprisingly fetching with her hair disheveled, though he preferred hair of straighter, silkier quality. Hers was thick, far too curly and slightly coarse. Yet none of this diminished her beauty. His gaze fell to her breasts. They were the perfect ripeness for the shape and size of her body, slightly more than a handful and not disproportionately large. He cradled the fullness of one. Her lashes lowered over her eyes as she breathed in his touch.

He reached over for the clamp and yanked it. Her eyes flew open and she gasped as the clamp snapped off her nipple, but she held onto the chain.

He rubbed the freed nipple and rolled it between his thumb and forefinger. Her eyelashes fluttered. He could not tell if his touch was aggravating the sensitive bud or enflaming her lust. Either way, he continued to fondle the nipple till she groaned. He removed the chain from her mouth and allowed it to dangle from the nipple, pulling the bud downward. Without the chain, she groaned more audibly.

He yanked on the chain, snapping the second clamp off, and allowed the set to clatter to the floor. Palming both breasts, he kneaded the supple orbs.

"Mmmm," she purred. "May I have your cock, Master?"

He rarely granted cock this early. A submissive had to earn it. With Miss Terrell, it was especially dangerous, for once he permitted her access, he relinquished control. She knew this. It was why she wanted his cock this soon.

"You have yet to deserve it," he replied.

"You gave it freely before."

He pinched a nipple and twisted it. Hard. Her cry heightened in pitch the more he twisted. He released the nipple. Panting, she stared at the floor with widened yes.

"I will have none of your sauciness, Miss Terrell."

"Yes, Master. Your pardon, Master."

If he had not established his dominance forcibly enough before, he would do it tonight. Staring at her stiff nipples, he thought of all the wicked things he could do with them. The possibilities made his cock throb.

His gaze traveled lower, down the smooth plane of her abdomen to her navel. It was wondrous how that small indentation enhanced the sensuality of the belly. Looking lower, he took in her mons and the triangle of hair there. He cupped her mound, and despite the lightness of his touch, she gasped. Desire had coiled tight and ardent in her. It satisfied him that he could arouse her to this state.

He slipped a finger between her folds. Her breath trembled as he curled his finger. Her wetness sent his own lust soaring. He did not fully understand how he came to have such a potent reaction to her. Was it a quality innate to her kind? He found that hard to believe, yet how else could he desire a woman who was wrong for him in so many ways?

With slow deliberation, he fondled her with the one finger. Her legs quivered. She moaned when he withdrew his finger.

"You've a fountain between your legs, Miss Terrell," he said, studying the copious amount of moisture upon his finger.

"You have made it so," she responded in a sultry manner. "If you wish, you may drink from it."

He raised his brows at her forwardness and placed the soaked finger at her lips. "First tell me how you taste."

She took his finger into her mouth. Desire pulsed in his groin at the sight of her lips closed about his finger. Her tongue lapped at the underside of his digit as she gently sucked, sending pulses directly to his cock. She sucked harder. Bracing himself against the urge to fuck her madly, he rotated his finger and explored the warm wetness of her mouth. He slid the entire length into her, and she sucked and licked at it in earnest.

"Mmmmm," she purred.

The sound resonated inside his cock. He withdrew and fit two fingers between her thighs. He caressed the moist, plump folds. She was sodden. Absolutely sodden. He took in a heady breath of her arousal. He felt for her clitoris and rubbed the length of his fingers along the wanton nub of pleasure.

"How may I please you, Master?"

One would think the question emblematic of her submission. But, taking in the luminescence of her eyes as she gazed up at him, he thought otherwise. Miss Terrell might have the outward appearance of submission, but she was not powerless. She asked to please him because she knew that once she started him down that path, he would be less inclined to deny her. Perhaps it pleased her to please him, too. Or it pleased her to know that she could arouse him. In that, she would always hold sway, and he wondered that he could ever truly dominate her.

"I may or may not grant you that favor," he replied as he continued to fondle her clitoris, amazed at its engorgement. He toyed with it, tugging and stroking till she trembled. Though he knew the answer, he asked of her, "Why do you wish to please me?"

"Because it would please me, Master."

"How so?"

"Because I adore your cock. I have tasted of your meat and drunken your seed, if you remember."

Remember? How could he ever forget?

"Since then," she continued between uneven breaths, "I have longed to feast once more upon you, to have you in my mouth, all of you, deep into my mouth and down my throat."

His own breath hitched. He continued to rub her between the legs as she painted her wanton vision.

"More than my mouth, however, my cunnie desires your cock. I would have you punish me with its hardness. Plunge it in my slit as far as it can go. I would I could take your cods into my cunnie."

His cock and balls ached, taking away his ability to think clearly. Of course, he had brought this upon himself. He should have known that giving her an inch would lead to a mile. His fingers, however, continued with their ministrations effortlessly.

"And then my arse would demand the same."

He shoved two fingers into her to quiet her. Her breath grew instantly ragged when he curled his fingers inside her furnace. How he longed to bury his cock into her soaking heat. As he found and caressed the most sensitive part of her cunnie, he drank in the look of lust upon her countenance. Her furrowed brow, her parted lips. She was not the only one who could command a reaction. Her lashes fluttered.

"M-Master…"

"What is it?" he prompted when she said no more.

"I…"

He made sure not to neglect her clitoris as he intensified his stroking of her cunnie.

"Oh, damn…I…"

"You wish to spend."

"Yes, Master."

"Desperately?"

The furrow of her brow deepened as she nodded.

"Say it."

"I d-desperately wish to spend."

"Master."

"Master."

Slowly, he withdrew his hand. She groaned at the loss.

"You wish me to beg for permission to spend, Master?"

"No, because I am not prepared to grant it, however nicely you may beg for it. You are being taught a lesson, Miss Terrell, for trifling with me. I cannot sanction your holding my properties hostage."

"The letter, you mean? But I never—"

She stopped herself. Surely she did not mean to deny that she had the letter?

"You will get the punishment you desire," he continued, "only you will come to rue it."

Chapter Ten

Damn.

Terrell trusted that Gallant did not have a mean streak in him, but how far would he go? Perhaps she should not have boasted of her ability to withstand any punishment he could mete out, especially when he had brought her body to such heightened aggravation so easily. She burned for his touch. What could she say or do to compel him to shove his fingers into her once more? How deliciously those digits had stroked her, his hand bumping and rubbing her most sensitive bud.

She knew now that he would not allow her to spend anytime soon. She knew now that she would first have to suffer the punishment he claimed she would rue. Gallant was not a cruel man, but he understood pain, and she did not doubt that he could be quite effective at torture if he were so inclined. Most of all, he seemed to know her body better than herself, knew just how to touch her to drive her to distraction. She had never before come across a man so skilled at arousing her.

She watched as he went to pick up the candle. Returning, he held the candle beside her. She felt the warmth of the small flame near her breast. Slowly he moved the candle below the orb, the top of the flame barely grazing her.

Her breathing became shallow. She had never been burned before, and hoped he had no intention of doing so. In Bridgetown, she had seen a female slave who had been burned. For days after, Terrell would retch whenever she recalled the charcoal coloring of the woman's skin, how it peeled away like paper to reveal the melted flesh below, how the hands were swollen yellow with infection.

Gallant must have seen the fear in her eyes for he promptly asked, "What is your safety word?"

She faltered. "I forgot."

His lips pressed into a displeased line. He fisted his free hand into her hair, yanking her head back. His gaze bored into her. "Fanny. Do not forget it."

"Yes, Master."

He released her and traced the curve of her breast with the tip of the candle flame. He did not linger long enough for the heat of the candle to cause any pain. Nonetheless, she exhaled in relief when he set the candle aside.

He crossed his arms. "Do you often forget your safety words when you are with others?"

"I've never needed to use a safety word before."

"But you've always had one."

"I suppose."

This seemed to anger him. "Suppose? You are required to have one, whether you use it or not."

She shrugged. "Not all members are as rigorous with the rules as you, Master Gallant."

"Then you must demand one. It is foolhardy not to have it at your disposal."

"Will I require one tonight?"

"If it will impress upon you its importance."

Her pulse raced at his response. His eyes had steeled, and she began to understand how she might not wish to trifle with him.

"On your knees, Miss Terrell," he instructed.

She complied without word. Her trepidation of the candle now gone, she was reminded of how her body yearned for his touch.

"Now lie face down."

She sat down first and lay upon her side before rolling onto her chest. She did not like the sensation of her breasts flattened into the floor. He pulled her up by the hips, causing more pressure upon her breasts. With his neckcloth, he wrapped her wrists, still bound together in the shirt, to her hips. Next, he pulled up her ankles and bound those to her wrists. She felt like a trussed calf, though a calf would not have to suffer so unnatural a position. With her back arched, her derriere in the air, all her weight rested upon her knees and her breasts, her hardened nipples pressing against a rug that did little to soften the wood floor beneath.

"I want you to keep this position at all times," Gallant said.

"Yes, Master."

She heard his footsteps retreat. With the side of her face against the floor, her vision was limited. He picked up something from the table. The crop perhaps.

"Ah!" she yelped as a sharp bite exploded upon her rump. It was the crop. It stung her again, this time on her thigh. Her body, as a matter of instinct, turned away from the cause of pain.

"Steady," he reminded her.

With a grimace, she forced her body back in place and promptly wished she had a flatter bosom.

He tapped the crop gently over the length of her other thigh and then her rump, preparing that side for the eventual blow.

Snap!

She cried out but maintained her position.

"Tell me, what is the most memorable punishment you have had?" he inquired.

"The one you are about to give."

As soon as she had spoken, she worried that he might consider her response a saucy one, though she meant it sincerely.

"Do not patronize me, Miss Terrell."

The crop cracked against the vaults of her feet. She cried out an oath.

"Miss Terrell, you will refrain from foul language. It is hardly appropriate in a submissive."

He struck her feet again. She shrieked, for though he had employed the same strength, the delivery hurt more. He rubbed the bottom of one foot with his thumb.

"The nerves here are especially sensitive and susceptible to pain," he explained.

She was still in a state of shock, for she had not been struck there before. She had once seen it done to another member at the Red Chrysanthemum and could not fathom the cries she had heard. Now she comprehended all too well.

She had mistakenly believed that Master Gallant would take a more gradual approach with her, as he had done with Miss Katherine, but why would he? She was not the neophyte that Miss Katherine was. And she had boasted one too many times of her abilities as a submissive.

"In Spain, they call this form of punishment *bastinado*. It has been in existence there since the 16th century. In China, it has existed for much longer. The Chinese civilization is quite impressive, though our modern society has long forgotten their contributions. If not for the Chinese, we would not have paper, the compass, or gunpowder."

He landed the crop against a foot again. She ground her teeth. Her eyes began to water. How was it her feet could not adapt to the pain? Each strike felt as if she were being hit for the first time.

"I'm waiting, Miss Terrell."

Her mind reeled. Waiting? For what?

Crack!

"Oh!" She suddenly remembered. "Thank you! Thank you, Master!"

"Much better."

To her relief, he applied the crop to her thighs and backside.

"Permission to speak, Master," she requested. She did not want the crop against her feet again.

"Granted."

"I spoke sincerely, Master. You are capable of rendering the most impressive of punishments."

"Indeed I am, and it is fully my intention to provide you an unforgettable one."

Chapter Eleven

From where he stood, Charles could see her profile. Her eyes had widened but there was no despair, only a healthy dose of fear. She had asked for this, after all.

He took a step back to admire her form. *My God.* She had the most luscious arse. Like ripe melons, the cheeks offered much to feast upon. They did not sag or wrinkle. They were fuller, more round than he had ever seen. They were certainly not small and meek but almost stately in size and shape.

His gaze traveled to her feet. The bottoms were of a lighter color than the rest of her and he could see the blush of the crop upon them. He ran a knuckle along the arch. She shivered. Raising the crop, he landed it against each foot in turn. She cried out, her body twisting, wanting to escape the crop but forced to endure it.

'Thank you, Master," she said through gritted teeth.

Pleased, he set aside the crop. He felt a twinge of guilt for not having warned her of the *bastinado*. With a new submissive, he ought to have taken his time to learn her background and make a gradual assessment of her tolerance. But he had decided to accept her bold assertions as the truth. And she needed to appreciate the importance of safety words. He knew he was attentive and would not overwhelm her, but the same could not be said of others.

He retrieved the candle next and held it over her rump. She saw the flame from the corner of an eye, and her body stiffened. He wondered at her response and held the candle at a distance, such that the melted wax would cool considerably before it landed. Nonetheless, she cried out when he titled the candle and allowed the wax to drop upon her back.

"What is your safety word, Miss Terrell?"

"I don't need it," she mumbled.

"What is it?"

"Fanny."

"Good." He lowered the candle a little and adorned a buttock. "Second to your punishment tonight, what has been the most memorable for you in your time at the Red Chrysanthemum?"

"They are nothing to speak of compared to yours."

"I require no flattery, Miss Terrell."

To add emphasis, he lowered the candle farther and splashed more wax upon her derriere. She gasped. It was a delicious sound. As with all her sounds, he heard it in his cock.

"I am not partial to the wiles of a coquette," he said. "Search your memory and provide me a memorable punishment."

He waited, but when she said nothing, he titled the candle.

"Mr. Cock!" she exclaimed.

"Mr. Cock?"

"It was not his real name, of course, but he insisted I call him that."

"And what manner of cock did he have?"

"The smallest little thing barely worth noting."

He lowered the candle. She gasped and squirmed as

droplets of hot wax splattered her backside.

"One thing I absolutely will not tolerate in a submissive is lying," he stated.

"It was quite long."

"Not all men place great stock in the comparison of their cocks."

Having said so, however, he felt a tug of jealousy thinking of a large cock inside of Miss Terrell.

"What punishment did Mr. Cock impose upon you?"

"He liked to place the pillow over my face while we fu—engaged in congress. At first it was diverting, but once, he held the pillow over me too long. I nearly fainted from want of breath."

Charles paled. "A safety word would have been useless, but did you have a signal, a gesture, that indicated you needed him to cease?"

"I cannot remember. I was too frightened. I clawed at his arms and saw afterward that I had even drawn blood, but there was a look in his eyes, as if he should have liked for me to suffocate and expire."

This was not what he wanted to hear. "Who was he?"

"I know not his real name."

"Was he a regular?"

"No. He was passing through town."

He shook his head. Joan needed to do better with whom she permitted to indulge in the Red Chrysanthemum.

"Did you have any further encounters with the man?"

"The following night, I was insistent that we not compromise my breath. He had no interest in me then."

Seeing that she was subtly moving her body from side to side to relieve the pressure upon her breasts, he nudged her body with his leg. "You may lie upon your side."

"Thank you."

"Breath play is exceptionally dangerous. You ought not engage in it lest you trust your partner without question."

"I would trust you, Master Gallant."

He glanced at her sharply. "After your frightful experience, you would dare attempt it again?"

She lowered her lashes in thought. "Perhaps not. But it was titillating at first. My nature is most wanton."

"Did you consider using the safety word when I dropped the wax upon you?"

"Only briefly."

"There is no shame in employing your safety word."

"I want to experience all that you would do to me."

She stared at him, determination flashing in her eyes. He found it difficult to swallow. Suddenly, he wanted to do everything to her, every wicked and lascivious act. He wanted to take her body to new heights, new triumphs.

He rolled her onto her back and knelt beside her, still holding the candle. Her gaze fixed upon the flickering flame with some fear. He insinuated his free hand between her thighs and began stroking. She moaned.

"Do not spend," he cautioned, stroking till she was sopping wet once more. He let hot wax fall upon her belly.

She caught her breath but her arousal remained undisturbed. He put his thumb at her clitoris and the next two fingers into her quim. She groaned long and low. His cock wanted to be where his fingers were, buried in her hot, wet paradise.

"Do not spend," he reminded as he fondled her. He dripped wax next to her navel, but what fear she had of the candle was overtaken by lust. He intensified his ministrations till she writhed and whimpered in her need for release. Her back arched. Her brow furrowed. She began panting heavily.

"Do not dare to spend without my permission," he warned, dropping wax upon a quivering breast. He could see the tension in her body from her head to her toes. She squeezed her eyes shut. "Don't spend, Miss Terrell."

"I can't," she said through clenched teeth.

"You will," he replied but fondled her faster.

"Then stop—!"

He pulled his hand from her abruptly.

Her mouth fell open as if he had struck her something fierce. She stared up into the rafters. He could see the turmoil in her countenance. She did not want to disappoint and flout his command, but her body wanted him to continue his sublime ministrations.

"Wait," she breathed. "Perhaps I…"

"You wish for more?"

"Yes, please."

"More of the candle as well?"

She nodded.

He obliged and decorated her body with more of the wax. She gasped but without fear this time.

"Well done," he praised.

Rising to his feet, he slid his foot beneath her derriere and rolled her back onto her front. She groaned as her breasts were once again pressed into the floor. He returned the candle to the table and observed the moisture glistening upon his other hand. His nose caught the whiff of her desire. He took in a deep breath. His cock had been hard long enough.

Chapter Twelve

S tay."

Terrell caught herself from replying, "Where am I to go?"

She heard him walking to the door, the door opening, and then the closing of the door. She was not happy to be back upon her breasts and knees and hoped he would not leave her, as he had once done, for half an hour. She wanted to spend, desperately. Her body was boiling with desire. Perhaps she should not have told him to stop. She had been on the verge of spending, his fondling having wreaked havoc upon her. What was the worst he could do if she disobeyed and spent?

But she did want to please him and prove she was worthy of his dominance. Her body was still perched upon the precipice. If she worked her cunnie, she could bring herself to spend in his absence. Surely he would not know, though she could not be certain. Gallant seemed far too attuned to her body. And she wanted to submit herself completely to him. He was the only man she completely trusted.

So she stayed where she was. Fortunately, he was not away for long. She heard him return and drop something soft but heavy upon the ground. She craned her neck to see.

Rope. He had gone to get rope.

She watched him throw the rope over one of the beams in the rafters. Her heart skipped a beat. After he had set up the ropes, he walked over and untied his neckcloth, releasing her ankles. He pulled her to her feet by the shirt, which he then disengaged from her arms. She welcomed the relief.

"Clasp your hands behind your head," he ordered.

She complied and breathed in anticipation as he wound a cord of rope about her chest, above her breasts. His skill with rope bondage exceeded any she had witnessed. She wanted him to touch her again. It was maddening having him so near but only feeling the slight brush of his fingers as he wrapped her.

"Permission to speak, Master."

"Granted," he replied as he wound rope beneath her breasts.

"From whom did you learn such art with the ropes? Was it Mistress Brownwen?"

"No one here. I came across a Japanese brothel in my travels."

A Japanese brothel. It sounded mysterious and exciting. She liked the look of concentration upon his physiognomy as he plied his craft.

"Where was this Japanese brothel?"

He looked at her oddly. "In Japan."

"And where is this Japan?"

"In the Orient. A much smaller country than China but no less proud. They certainly would not admit to being intimidated by their larger neighbor."

Gallant had been to the Orient. She had never met someone who had been there, though she had once seen an Oriental from afar.

"Why were you in Japan?"

He secured one of the dangling ropes to the rope at her back. "Because I had a reckless curiosity to know a society so different from ours."

"Reckless?"

"Foreigners of our kind are forbidden in Japan. China, too, save for the factory in Canton. Anyone found aiding a foreigner is punished with death."

"Yet you managed."

"I had Wang, an extremely capable and devoted guide, as well as much silver upon me."

He proceeded to wind a new cord of rope about her hips, standing close enough to her that she could smell him. She knew not what it was, but he had an intoxicating scent. She leaned toward him. Her nipples nearly touched him. He slowed his movement and stared down at her. She returned his gaze.

Touch me.

She saw desire burning in his eyes, but he merely continued circling her hips with the rope. She breathed in deeply. "Tell me of this Japanese brothel."

"It was unlike any brothel. What they accomplished with rope made the female form truly exquisite."

Having seen his handiwork upon Mistress Scarlet, she understood the appreciation. "I wish I could see the brothel for myself. I wonder how they came to use bondage for such titillating purposes?"

"The practice of *kinbaku* was first employed to restrain, humiliate and torment prisoners."

"It is a most lovely torment then."

"You may think differently when we are done."

He tied another one of the hanging ropes to the binding about her hips, then pulled the rope to hoist her hips up toward the rafters. She found her body, save for her legs, parallel to the floor. Her toes dangled a few inches into the air. It was an extraordinary sensation. Whereas the ropes encasing her gave her at once a sense of constraint and security, the suspension made her feel utterly helpless. The weight of her body pressed into the ropes.

He took her left ankle and bound it to her thigh. She felt her heel nestled against her rump. He did the same with the other ankle and secured both ankles to the last rope hanging from the beams above. She felt some relief with the addition of the third supporting point. Walking toward her head, he pulled her arms behind her, bent them at the elbows and wrapped his neckcloth about her forearms. Then he stepped back to admire his efforts.

She wished she could see herself tied and suspended in rope. It felt wondrous. It was as close to flying as she would ever come. And the ropes were an extension of *him*. She would rather his hands wrapped her body, but the ropes sufficed beautifully in their absence. She wanted to know how else a woman might be bound and suspended, for she wanted more. Her cunnie pulsed.

"May I have your cock now?" she asked, noticing the outline of his erection. "I am at the perfect height."

"Not yet," he murmured and returned to stand behind her. He pulled and adjusted the rope securing her hips, raising them higher than her head.

She preferred the prior position but had no time to complain, for his hand was between her thighs, fondling her clitoris. She moaned. After fingering the nub, he always managed to find the most sensitive parts. He plied the spots till she panted and quivered. It did not take her body long to climb the cliff of ecstasy. If only he would allow her to fall over the precipice...

But she feared he would not—yet. To her dismay, he retracted his hand all too soon. She heard a rustling sound, and then her dear little bud, aroused and teased to the brink, was being pinched by something hard and metal. Perhaps one of the clamps he had affixed to her nipple earlier. To her surprise, it did not hurt as much as her nipples had. Then she felt a decidedly uncomfortable tugging upon her clitoris.

The clamp had a weight dangling from it.

He gave her a gentle shove, and as she swayed, so did the weight, pulling her sensitive nub to and fro. She heard him pick up an article from the floor and wondered what further wickedness he would attempt. He flicked her clitoris a few times, then stroked the folds between her legs.

Fuck me, she silently groaned. *Fuck me with those long capable fingers.*

But he only teased her with the prospect. His fingers would only graze the insides of her nether lips. Her cunnie clenched, wanting to suck his fingers into her. The tension twisting in her belly was unbearable.

At last he inserted a finger. Her ravenous cunnie grasped at it, starving for more. He inserted a second finger and stroked her. She felt herself scaling the cliff in leaps and bounds. The precipice was so near!

But he withdrew once more. She could not see what he was doing. She did not care. If only he would replace his fingers, he could do anything he wished.

"You have not been given permission to spend," he reminded her. "You must refrain a while longer."

Longer? How much longer? She swallowed with difficulty as he sank his fingers into her. Now she wished he would not. But he felt divine. Too divine. She had yearned for him to be inside her, but now that he was, she preferred the opposite. She was damned either way.

His fingers moved inside her, and it took all her concentration not to fall into the climax she so desperately desired.

He removed his fingers and nudged the weight upon her clitoris to sway. Closing her eyes, she took in a deep and ragged breath. Her cunnie was a boiling mess of arousal. But she was determined to succeed. She would not spend until she had his permission.

"Ready, Miss Terrell?"

She nodded, tensing as his fingers entered her. *Oh, God. Oh, God. Oh, God.* She could think of nothing more difficult than her current task. The intensity of it…she wanted to cry.

Slowly, he dragged his fingers out. Even when he was completely out, she had to still her body from succumbing. It was easier spending the day sowing the fields in Barbados. She sensed him wiping her wetness upon something. There was a pause, and then she knew what it was. Something hard and smooth slid into her anus.

She cried out, not because the intrusion produced any pain. The diameter of it was narrow and it had been coated with her wetness, but the wealth of sensation nearly sent her over the edge. He nestled the implement farther into her arse. Her teeth chattered as she tried to keep herself from spending. Her rectum could accommodate more, but it was the first time he had touched her there. And it was…beyond magnificent.

The intrusion was a hook with a blunted end. She could feel the straight part pressing upon her backside. It must have also had a rope attached to it for he yanked her toward the hook and tied it so that any drop in her head pulled upon the hook in her arse.

She decided then that she wanted an end to her torment. She was completely defenseless, unable to employ her arts of seduction, to bend him to her will. Instead, she was completely at his disposal, her body his to do whatever he wished. And he had chosen to deny her that which she craved above all else at the moment. She wondered that she could endure any more.

Chapter Thirteen

She was a feast for the eyes. Her naked body, still adorned with the candlewax, trussed in the beauty of rope, hanging helplessly in the air, a small iron weight dangling from her pleasure bud, a silver hook cleaving her arse.

Charles rubbed his crotch. He could not keep her in suspension for much longer, for she was not yet trained to endure great lengths. There were many other forms of suspension he could put her through. He considered hanging her by her bosom, or upside down by the ankles—or perhaps he would have her legs spread that he might toy with her cunnie. He could drive himself mad with such visions.

From where he stood, he could see the distress upon her profile. The tension in her body was palpable, and he was tempted to provide it relief. If he pushed his fingers into her once more, she would surely spend. But he reminded himself that she held his letter hostage.

How many times had she used her wiles to force his hand? After tonight, she would never consider such mischief again.

He would, however, provide her a different manner of relief. Taking up the crop, he whipped it against her thigh. She jumped. He needed to ease her down from the precipice upon which she dangled. Pain would aid her. He struck the vaults of her feet. She squealed but did not employ her safety word. He flicked the crop all over her body. Her belly. Her breasts. The inside of her thigh. She yelped when the crop landed on her cunnie.

"Thank you, Master."

Hearing the words was too much. He could not deny his own desires for any longer. "You have done well, Miss Terrell, and have earned your cock."

Her eyes lit up. He undressed slowly for he needed to gather himself. If he took her too soon, he would spend before he wanted.

"Thank you, Master. My cunnie has ached for your cock, for its hardness to fuck me into submission."

Lust roared in his cock. She was not helpless, he decided. Not while she still had her mouth. He made a silent note to gag her next time.

Having shed his collar and shirt, his braces hanging from his waist, he went to stand before her. He caressed her bottom lip with his thumb. "And where might you like your cock?"

"In my cunnie, but my mouth would delight in it, too."

She looked up at him with eyes he was finding far too irresistible. He went to stand behind her.

"Cunnie it is."

He undid his fall. His cock sprang forth, hungry. Nay, starving. Had he ever craved cunnie this desperately?

He adjusted the hook for good measure. She grunted. Holding his cock, he pressed it against her entry. Once his tip felt her moist heat, he could delay no further.

He plunged himself into her. He had to close his eyes against the brilliance surrounding his length. Such incredible heat. Such copious wetness. He sank himself farther. If he had not years of practice withholding himself, he could easily have spent in seconds, especially as her cunnie flexed about him, greedily grasping his meat.

He withdrew his cock, relishing how his flesh slid against hers, how her cunnie pulled at the flare of his crown. He pushed himself back in.

"Mmmmm," she sighed.

Holding her in place by the buttocks, he began a measured thrusting, at times burying himself to the hilt, till he could feel the curve of the hook at his groin. She seemed to enjoy the fullness the most.

"Do you wish to spend first, Master?"

"First?" he responded, mesmerized by the sight of his cock appearing then disappearing into her most intimate place. "That presumes you will have the chance to spend."

She started. "Will...will I not?"

"Do you promise to behave from now on? At all times?"

"I promise!"

"Should I believe your promise?"

She was silent. He increased the tempo of his thrusts. She moaned and struggled a little against the ropes.

"I-I've learned my lesson, M-Master."

He shoved himself into her hard. She groaned. For a moment, her head dipped down, but it tugged upon the hook and she quickly righted herself.

"Have you?"

He thrust into her more relentlessly. Her cunnie had ceased clenching his cock, and he sensed the tension in the whole of her body. She would spend if he allowed her.

"Yes! Yes! Please let me spend."

He slowed his motions and withdrew. She groaned in despair, and he felt himself a cad, but, alas, he was not wholly convinced of her promises. He admired the sheen of her wetness upon his cock. *Damnation*. He wanted to permit her to spend. He enjoyed the look of her overcome with rapture.

But she needed this set-down. The panther needed to be tamed. If she was ever to be his submissive.

He went to stand before her and pointed his cock at her mouth. She took him in with eagerness and devoured his length as if she had not eaten in days. Several oaths went through his mind. There was no mouth more marvelous than hers. It amazed him how well she swallowed his erection. She must have taken in cocks much longer than his.

She sucked her own nectar off his cock, but the movement of her head was limited by the hook. He compensated by thrusting his hips, slowly at first, and then faster, his cods swinging against her chin, when he could resist no more. Her mouth was pure heaven. The heat roiling in his cods and flaring in his groin collected into his cock. Holding the back of her head, he plunged himself in deep. The hairs of his pelvis pressed into her nose. With a roar, he released his load.

Stars seemed to burst in his head as he bucked against her, shoving his cock as deep as she would take him. Or deeper. Her body jerked against the bonds as she gagged. Greedily, he thrust into her one last time before providing her relief. A last spurt of seed landed upon her cheek and lips. With a violent shudder, he stumbled and shook his head. *My God.*

He stared at her, at the dollop of his mettle upon her mouth. How was it she could produce such carnal rhapsody?

She licked his seed from her lips. "Is Master pleased?"

Unable to speak, he nodded. After a few minutes, he replaced his cock and the fall of his pants. He slid on his shirt and pulled up his braces. Then he set about untying her from the rafters. He removed the hook from her arse first, then the clamp upon her clitoris. He untied her ankles and lowered her hips so that she could stand, then he undid the ropes one by one. Last came his neckcloth.

"You look quite fetching in men's linen," he whispered into her ear.

Having spent, he found himself in a good mood.

"Are we done, Master?"

"Not quite."

Picking up two strands of rope, he wrapped each of her wrists.

"Lie down upon the bed," he instructed.

He took in her backside as she went to the bed, drinking in the sight of her supple derriere before daring to look at her marred back. She lay upon the bed face up. He secured her wrists to opposite posts of the bed, then did the same to her ankles, spreading her wide.

After retrieving a calming poultice, he sat down beside her. He reached beneath her arse to apply the poultice. "Did you enjoy the candle wax?"

"Yes, Master."

"The *bastinado*?"

"Not at all."

"And the *kinbaku*?"

"A great deal."

He rubbed the poultice upon the bottoms of her feet and up her legs. She whimpered when his hand caressed the inside of a thigh. He could feel the heat emanating from her cunnie. Putting aside the poultice, he cupped her mons and stroked the hair there. He dipped his fingers lower.

"Ohhh," she crooned.

Enjoying his effect upon her, he pressed two of his fingers into her cunnie. She was still soaking wet. Her cunnie tightened about him.

"Oh, yes," she mumbled as he sawed his fingers in and out.

She writhed against the bed and angled her hips to compel his fingers deeper. He added a third and gyrated his digits against her.

"Oh, yes, oh, God. Am I...am I allowed to spend?"

"Not yet, my dear." His heartbeat quickened as he contemplated how her slit stretched to accommodate his fingers. "What is your safety word?"

She was straining against her bonds, clenching her hands.

"Your safety word, Miss Terrell."

"Hmm?"

He ceased and began withdrawing his fingers. "Safety word."

"Fanny," she murmured.

He inserted his fingers, this time fitting all four and his thumb. Her wet cunnie swallowed him easily. Her mouth fell open, and her eyes rolled to the back of her head. His heart pounded as he stared at how his hand had disappeared into her. Thankfully he had already spent or his arousal would be shooting through the roof.

"Do you require your safety word?" he asked hoarsely.

She made no reply.

"Answer me."

"No...but let me spend."

He rotated his hand. He had not intended to insert it fully into her, but something about this woman prompted him to the edge. He thought of "Mr. Cock", and it pleased him to think that he now might be stretching her cunnie more than it had ever been stretched before.

"Please let me spend," she begged.

"Before I let you spend, I want my letter, Miss Terrell."

She whimpered. "But I don't have it."

He moved his hand inside of her. "What do you mean?"

"I—Miss Sarah has it."

He frowned. She had made Miss Sarah an accomplice in her mischief?

"That is unfortunate," he said, pulling out his hand.

"No! Please, Master Gallant."

He wiped the moisture from his hand onto her belly. Standing, he collected his remaining articles of clothing.

"You do not understand," she protested.

"When I have my letter in hand, I will send someone to untie you."

"No! Wait!"

He left her before he changed his mind. He cursed himself. A part of him could deny her nothing, wanted to give her the greatest pleasure he could. The other insisted he prevail. She ought not involve others. He recalled his anger at how readily she had offered herself to Wendlesson, his outrage at how she had forced herself upon him and how he had, in the end, submitted to her. Perhaps he had not truly forgiven her yet.

"Master Gallant!"

Miss Sarah greeted him at the bottom of the stairs. She took in his disheveled appearance and state of partial dress. "I take it you found Miss Terrell."

"She said you have the letter."

"Yes, she gave it to me for safekeeping."

"Safekeeping?"

"Yes. I suppose she feared she might misplace it. I

meant to give it to you earlier, but I thought you might want to, er, speak with Terrell first."

Miss Sarah held out the letter.

He accepted it. "You intended to give it to me upon my arrival?"

"Yes. Is something amiss?"

Though he knew the letter he held was the one he sought, he turned it over nonetheless to see the Brentwood name. He let out a breath and shook his head. Why did she do it?

"Is something amiss?"

"I have merely realized I was under a misapprehension," he answered Miss Sarah. "Thank you for the letter."

Giving her a bow, he turned and headed back up the stairs. At the threshold of the room he had just left, he paused. He was not a man prone to misjudgment, yet he seemed to commit them with some frequency at the Red Chrysanthemum. First with Miss Greta. Now with Miss Terrell. He opened the door and stepped in.

To no surprise, Miss Terrell was where he had left her, tethered to the bed. He took in her shapely limbs, the swell of her hips, and breasts that did not seem to flatten or slide to the sides. Something about her proportions, the ratio of bosom to waist to hips to thighs, enflamed his blood. As compelling—nay, more compelling—than the greatest works of art.

She lifted her head and looked at him briefly before lying back down. "I take it you have your letter, Master Gallant."

Sauntering toward her, he replied, "I have. And I owe you an apology, Miss Terrell."

She stared up at the ceiling with a wry half-grin. "Hang

your apology and fuck me."

With pleasure, he thought to respond. But he was not about to take commands from her. He set his articles down and sat upon the bed.

"Why did you let me believe you guilty of extortion?"

"It was an unexpected opportunity, of sorts."

She had the pouncing ability of a panther. He surveyed the landscape of her body and grasped a breast. "Did the opportunity yield what you had hoped?"

She smiled. "That and more, Master."

He fondled the orb he held.

"Did you return to torment me more?" she inquired, sucking in her breath when he passed his thumb over her nipple.

"With pleasure," he replied, and, settling between her legs, lowered his head to her cunnie.

She tensed in surprise, but relaxed when he caressed the insides of her thighs. Her musk was heady in his nostrils, the smell of desire stoking his cock. He flicked his tongue at her clitoris, and her body bowed off the bed. He would enjoy feasting upon her.

"Will you let me spend, Master?" she asked.

"But I have barely begun."

"Yes, but I wish to know if I am to leash my arousal and hold it at bay?"

"You will be permitted to spend."

She sighed in relief, and he returned his attention to her delightful cunnie. The coloring was distinctively pink compared to the brown of her skin. He pried the folds apart with able fingers to better access her engorged clitoris. He licked at the swollen bud. She shivered. He drew his tongue languidly along its sides, flicked the pearl at the center, till he found the spot that elicited her greatest groans and longest moans.

"Thank you, Master, thank you."

He took her clitoris into her mouth and sucked.

"Unh," she gasped.

He released her, and her body heaved. Her legs quivered.

"Please tend to me more, Master."

Obliging, his tongue began its assault upon her in earnest. She writhed against her bonds. He held her still by the thighs.

"*Oh, Lord*," she cried.

He slowed before ceasing his ministrations completely. Perplexed, she tugged at the ropes. Rising, he went to sit beside her hip. She looked at him with a worried brow.

"I thought you—I thought I was to spend," she said.

"You shall. When I am ready for you to spend."

He could smell her desire upon him, still taste her in his mouth. It made the heat swirl in his groin like a caged tiger seeking release. He had to admit she had done well refraining from spending. Better than he might have done, had he been in her situation. But while he intended to atone for his mistake, he was still the Master and she the submissive.

Looking her over, his heartbeat quickened. She had a body made for *fucking*. The devil could not have done a finer job molding such a temptation. Leaning over a breast, he captured the nipple in his mouth. She voiced a trembling moan as he suckled the dark brown peak. He alternated between light caresses of the tongue and concentrated sucking. She lifted her hips, her cunnie undoubtedly aching for attention.

"Please…" she murmured.

He sucked her nipple hard as he snaked two fingers

between her legs. She cried out, and her body pressed into him, into his mouth, into his fingers. He devoured the nipple with his mouth as his fingers entered her.

"Please!" she exclaimed. "Let me..."

He ought to. She deserved it. But a small part of him still wanted to impress upon her his dominance.

"*Please.*"

He could not make her beg any more. Sitting upright, for he wanted to watch her face as she spent, he agitated his fingers furiously inside her.

"Spend, my dear, spend."

With a cry that seemed to roll from deep within her, her body shattered. She thrashed madly against the bed, her head craned back, and a stream of fluid sprang from between her legs. He continued to pump his fingers inside her slit. More wetness spurted from her. She seemed to spend for minutes upon end.

When he withdrew his fingers, she was still shaking. He did not often part from a woman till he knew that she had eased back to the grounds after being shot into the heavens, but he could not wait this time. Slipping from his braces, he threw off his shirt, climbed over her leg, let fall his trousers and plunged his cock into her.

How glorious she felt. How wet. How hot.

He bucked his hips, shoving himself deeper into her. He did not know if she might be too sensitive to bear the stimulation, but she angled her hips as best she could to receive him. Twisting around, he untied the ropes from her ankles. He swept his arms beneath her knees and brought her legs up beside her rib cage, opening up more of her cunnie for his penetration.

"Yes, fuck me, Charles, fuck me," she said.

His name upon her lips proved more provocative than

even that of Master. He drove his cock as far into her cunnie as he could, his cods slapping against her derriere, with a mad desperation to possess her through his cock. The sight of her, of lust sparkling in her eyes, her bosom bouncing with each and every thrust, her legs curled at her sides, all conspired to make him drill his cock into the depths of her womanhood.

She cried out when he thrust into her more roughly than he'd intended. He slowed his movements to allow her to catch up to him. Putting his thumb at her clitoris, he stroked her. Her cunnie clenched about him. He stroked her more as he rolled his hips.

"Harder," she gasped.

He obliged and rammed his cock into her. The bed struck the wall behind them. Tightly, she grasped the ropes about her wrists.

"Harder," she urged.

There was no turning back now. Propping his hands on either side of her, he pounded his cock into her, shoving her body into the bed and the bed into the wall.

"*Ye Gods*," she wailed above the smacking of his flesh upon hers. The bed banged against the wall loud enough that surely they could be heard two floors down.

And then her cunnie spasmed about his cock. Her lashes fluttered violently as her head was thrown back. Her body quaked and her legs flailed. Her wetness drenched his pelvis. Despite having spent earlier, he could not hold back and poured his seed deep inside of her, bucking several more times before shudders overtook his body.

He collapsed atop her. The drumming of his heart, the sound of their gasps for air, drowned out all else.

Mother of God. If one could go blind from the force of one's congress, he was as near to it as one could be.

He stayed inside her pulsing heat, his cock throbbing. Wrapped in her womanly warmth, he could not think of a more pleasurable place and wondered that he would ever want to move from her.

After he had collected his breath, he propped himself to look upon her. Her lashes resting against her cheek, her lips parted, her bosom still heaving in deep breaths, the glisten of perspiration upon her skin, an aura of contentment upon her countenance, her hair a mess. She could not look more beautiful.

As if sensing his gaze, she opened her eyes, and he was instantly struck by their brightness.

"Have I pleased you, Master?" she asked with uncharacteristic softness.

He brushed away a tendril of her hair matted to her temple. "Yes, Miss Terrell, you did well."

"Better than you expected?"

"Yes," he acknowledged. "I admit I had little faith at the start."

"Perhaps you will henceforth not underestimate me?"

Her cunnie squeezed his softened cock. She was right. He underestimated her at his peril.

"And you, I," he responded, pinching one of her nipples and twisting it.

She gasped loudly.

"That was for speaking my given name without permission," he explained.

He eased himself from her. Her wetness coated the hairs at his pelvis. He knew few women who ejaculated, and he was eager to witness it once more with Miss Terrell. It was madness.

He untied the ropes from her wrists and rubbed her chafed wrists. A wicked part of him hoped the blushing impressions would remain there to remind her of him.

"Thank you, Master," she said.

He met her stare and found himself pulled into the blackness of her pupils. Cupping the back of her head, he tilted her mouth up to receive his kiss. Their lips entwined tenderly, and he would have kissed her longer but for the spark of life in his cock. It was like a ravenous dog in her presence. Not wanting to wake the beast, he pulled away from her.

"Do you require more of the poultice?" he asked as he surveyed her body.

She grinned. "Not for tonight."

"Impish wench."

He gave her nipple a playful tweak. With a yelp, she bounded off the bed. She picked up his shirt.

"May I dress you, Master?"

He slid off the bed and found his handkerchief. After wiping himself, he pulled up his trousers. His pants had a wet spot about the thigh, though the bed had taken the majority of her fluids.

"You may punish me next time for soiling your pants," she offered, though she looked upon the dampness with a small smile.

God. Was there to be a "next time"?

"Be careful what you wish for, Miss Terrell," he cautioned as he received his shirt from her and pulled it overhead.

She knelt before him and buttoned his fall. "Your punishments only amplify my hunger."

He wondered if that could be true. Could she be that insatiable? Knowing how quickly his own lust had grown, he found the thought a little daunting. Yet he was not without curiosity about the answer.

After he had donned his waistcoat and she had tied his cravat to the best of her abilities, he took a turn at dressing her, though pulling the shirt upon her was hardly a task.

"Who cares for the rooms?" he asked, noting there were no liquid refreshments.

"Miss Anne."

"You ought partake of a beverage and replenish lost fluids."

"I can tend to my thirst later."

"You will tend to it now."

Surprised, she raised her brows. "If you insist, but why?"

"To keep your body in balance." Realizing he was speaking of an Oriental notion, he added, "That is an order."

Just then the candle flame, having reached the end of the wick, extinguished, leaving the room in darkness save what moonlight crept through the window.

"I shall obtain another candle," Miss Terrell said.

"You will first see that you partake of a beverage," he said, "then inform Anne that this room needs tending to."

"What of you, Master Gallant?"

"I will take care of myself." He took her by the arm and led her to the door. "The hour is late."

"Not for the Red Chrysanthemum."

"Nevertheless, I should take my leave."

"Shall you return tomorrow night?"

He opened the door. "Perhaps not. I have much to do."

"For your election?"

"Yes."

She paused upon the threshold. "I hope I have pleased you enough, Master, that you will consider returning."

"None of your cunning, Miss Terrell. My attendance tomorrow night, or lack thereof, has nothing to do with your performance. As I've said, I have much business to conduct. Now behave and fetch yourself something to drink."

"Yes, Master."

Leaning against the doorframe, he watched her amble down the hallway, observing the slight sway of her arse and those lovely naked legs.

Her scent was still upon him, and he was glad to have its company on the ride home. He wanted to return tomorrow night. He wanted to indulge in all manner of delicious depravity with Miss Terrell.

But it was wiser not to. She was fast becoming more addictive than opium.

Chapter Fourteen

C harles," a woman called to him as he accepted his gloves and hat from Baxter.

Charles turned to face the proprietress of the Red Chrysanthemum.

"I will have a word with you, if you please," she said. To Baxter, she asked, "Is Master Gallant's horse saddled?"

"I believe so," Baxter returned.

"Then I shall not be long. Come, Charles."

Charles, noting that she led him to her chambers and not to the parlor where she sometimes conducted business, deduced that she wanted more privacy with which to chastise him.

"Have a seat, *mon cheri*," she directed after she had eased herself onto a sofa. Though the fashion of the time had done away with panniers, Joan kept the more plentiful undergarments of prior decades.

"I am at your service, madam," he said before taking the settee opposite her.

She took in his appearance and was clearly pleased with what she beheld. "Perhaps I had been hasty in granting your freedom."

"Alas, I will be making no more wagers at the Red Chrysanthemum. Lady Luck does not favor me here."

She eyed his poorly tied cravat and disheveled hair. "I wonder that you do not make your own luck. I am pleased, of course, that you are returned tonight. I had a lovely new member tonight, a widowed duchess, whom I might have saved for you if I had known you would be here, but, pray tell, who compels your presence?"

He kept her gaze. "You've no wish to know."

The playfulness left her features as she considered the possibilities. "You will not take me into your confidence? Have I overestimated our friendship?"

"It is because I value your integrity that I risk our friendship. Trust me, madam. Ignorance is the wiser course."

He could see that she was tempted to speak the name of Miss Terrell, but he would not confirm an answer, that she would not be compelled to speak falsely if queried on the matter.

"I do trust you, Charles," she said at last. "It is because I trust you that I have a tremendous favor to ask of you."

"I should be happy to assist you in any way possible."

"I received a letter from my sister's house in Kingsborough today. She is ill, and her husband away, not likely to return for a sennight."

"I am sorry to hear it. How ill is she?"

"My sister is prone to fevers, but I mean to go to her. She is the youngest in our family and accustomed to being cared for. I think she will be quite despondent with only the servants to attend her. I wish to depart in the morning, and I wish to leave the Red Chrysanthemum in your charge during my absence."

She took his silence to indicate his reluctance and continued, "There is no other member I can think of who is up to the task, capable enough to run the inn whilst I am away."

"You honor me, Joan," he replied, "and pay me no

small compliment with this request, but I think you know my situation with the election—"

"I know, and it grieves me to impose upon you in such fashion when you must be busy, but in all my time as proprietress, I have never once handed the reins to anyone. It has taken me years to make the Red Chrysanthemum what it is."

"You have ruled it well."

She nodded. "And any lapse in governance, however brief, could take thrice as long to rebuild."

He had to agree with her assessment. Destruction was always easier, took less time, than construction.

"I would make every accommodation to ease your situation. You would have access to all my staff, and you could have my chambers to reduce the amount of travel."

He sat up. "I have not been long returned here."

"Only the members have changed during your time in the Orient. The rules are the same. I need someone to review new members, oversee the protocols each night, and maintain order. For someone of your capabilities, the tasks are simple. In the wrong hands, however, the consequences can be disastrous."

"I think you place too much trust in my person," he said, thinking once more of Miss Terrell.

She smiled in sympathy. "Of course you are merely mortal, *mon cheri,* and a man at that. I do not expect that you will be perfect, but I can think of no one who will take his responsibilities as seriously as you. In this vein, you will make an exceptionally fine MP."

He hesitated. He wanted to grant Joan this favor, but taking her place would necessitate him being at the Red Chrysanthemum daily. He would have no reprieve from Miss Terrell.

Which would be too great a temptation for the most stoic of men.

"I would not apply to you, truly," Joan said, "if I had any other viable options to turn to."

"I am not worthy of the responsibility."

Rising, she went to sit beside him. "Whatever transgression you think yourself guilty of cannot be so monumental. As governor of the Red Chrysanthemum, you can make the rules as you see fit. I give you free rein to do as you please."

"There is no one else? What of James?"

"He is returned home with his wife."

"Wendlesson?"

"Even were he capable enough, he would not be here for the whole sennight. You, Charles, are my only answer. If you do not accept, I could not go to Kingsborough."

He blew out a long, low breath. He could not be the reason she did not attend an ailing sister. "Very well."

She sighed in relief and grasped his hand. "*Merci, mon cheri, merci.* Thank you."

He kissed her hand. "*Avec plaisir.* I hope you will not doubt our friendship now."

"Of course not! And I should be at your disposal should you ever require a favor of me. I promise now to grant it."

He would have thought her promise foolhardy, but he knew it unlikely he would ask too great a favor, if any.

"My chambers will be ready for you by tomorrow night, and I will inform everyone tonight that they are to abide by your wishes, heed every dictate, every whim of yours."

Mischief seemed to twinkle in her eyes.

"I am being given *carte blanche* authority?" he asked,

though he knew he would not abuse his power.

"*Carte blanche, mon cheri.*"

He pressed his lips into a firm line. There was no escaping Miss Terrell now.

Chapter Fifteen

I would not attempt a darkie. I heard tell their cunnies emit the foulest odor."

In far too happy a mood, Terrell swept, without word, past Sophia and her patron for the evening. Sophia could accuse her all she wished. Her cunnie held Master Gallant's seed. Knowing this, she wanted nothing more at the moment.

Unable to resist, he had plunged his cock into her depths. To have him buried deep inside of her was nothing short of marvelous. The fury in which he'd pommeled into her cunnie made her feel his cock through the whole of her body. If she were not so aroused, it would have hurt. Indeed, her cunnie still ached from the pounding, but she relished the soreness. She would not sleep tonight for she would recount in her mind every moment with him.

She stopped by her room first to don more appropriate attire. Tonight, she wanted to draw no attention to herself. Tonight, she belonged to Master Gallant. Miss Sarah and George were in the room, the latter on his feet, holding on to the bed while reaching for the wooden toy upon the floor. Unable to attain the desired object, he squealed till Sarah bent down and picked it up for him.

"How was your evening with Master Gallant?" Sarah asked.

Terrell embraced herself and could not resist beaming.

"My word," Sarah responded, "I wonder I have ever seen you this happy?"

Terrell unpinned her hair and shook out her curls. "Master Gallant is most, shall we say, masterful."

"Hmm. That I suspected. I knew you would have your way with him, did I not?"

A knock at the door interrupted their colloquy.

"Master Richards requests an audience for his display," the maidservant Tippy informed them, "after which Madame will make an announcement."

"Will you attend?" Terrell asked Sarah after Tippy had left.

"I must put Georgie to bed first."

"Though I doubt the performance can top that of Master Gallant, I shall attend. I feel far too spirited at the moment to rest here."

"I wonder what announcement Madame intends to make?"

Terrell removed her shirt and reached for a shift. "Perhaps she means to chastise us for leaving *French letters* about."

George dropped his toy and squalled once more till Sarah picked it up for him.

"You ought give him the chance to retrieve it for himself," Terrell said.

"I suppose, but I am loath to have him cry. Madame was kind enough to permit me to keep him here with me, but she was adamant that he not fuss and distract the members. Is Master Gallant gone for the evening?"

"Alas, yes, and unlikely to return tomorrow."

"He must have many demands upon his time."

"Yes, but men will find the time to satisfy their carnal demands, come what may. I think Master Gallant does not desire me enough."

Even as she spoke, she recalled the fiery passion in his eyes and the force with which he had pounded his cock into her.

"Or he has more forbearance than most men," Sarah said as she laced the stays for Terrell. "I think he has a great sense of responsibility. It is a noble quality."

"Nevertheless, I wish he had less of it."

Sarah chuckled. "Nevertheless, you are a lucky skirt to have his attentions at the moment. You will want to make the most of it till Sir Arthur returns."

Lost in thought, Terrell only murmured, "Yes."

"Or perhaps you mean to give up Sir Arthur?"

Terrell selected her other gown of pale blue. It was a dress she had bought in her time with Sir Fairchild. Lady Fairchild had not allowed her to depart the apartment Sir Fairchild had kept for her with anything but her clothes, most of which she had had to sell to subsist.

"I cannot," Terrell responded. "It is plain that I am nothing more than a dalliance for Master Gallant."

"Do you wish for more than a dalliance?"

Terrell thought for several minutes as she dressed before replying, "No. I cannot afford more with Master Gallant as I have not demanded any compensation from him."

"He is a gentleman with means. He could afford to pay you."

Terrell shook her head emphatically. "I do not wish him to. He has not the wealth I require."

"And if he did?"

Terrell would not permit herself to think on such fancies. Of course she would take Charles if he had the funds to sustain her. She would take him over any man.

"Serving as an MP does not net a man riches," Terrell said.

"No, but there are many posts to be had, many appointments that pay in the thousands, yet require little work."

"But Char—Master Gallant—must keep a good face and win friends and respect. He has not the luxuries of Sir Arthur, who can choose any mistress he desires, even a blackamoor, without losing his standing."

Sarah sighed in agreement. "Life can be most unfair."

Terrell thought of the slaves she had left behind in Barbados. Unfair was an understatement. Deserving or not, she had been blessed. She had been taken to England. She had her freedom whilst she remained. She intended to make the most of what providence had gifted her. If she could become the mistress of someone like Sir Arthur and took greater care of her allowance, she could assure herself a life of comfort.

"The dress becomes you," Sarah said after they had fixed her motley curls atop her head.

"I had best head down so as not to miss Madame's announcement."

"Please inform her that I will be in attendance as soon as Georgie is asleep."

Terrell glanced in the small looking glass upon the sideboard before departing. Perhaps she would indulge in buying a new ribbon to replace the old one upon her dress. Despite the old ribbon and the faded hue of the dress, she felt pretty. She also felt sore in many places on her body: her arse, cunnie and nipples. But they were reminders of Master Gallant.

Downstairs in the parlor, where demonstrations and performances took place, there was a small stage a few inches high. It was upon this stage that Terrell was first captivated by Master Gallant, how he had commanded the submission of Mistress Scarlet.

An audience of nearly two dozen members had already assembled in the room, and Terrell took a seat in the back row. Upon the stage stood Master Richards and his submissive, a fair young nymph whom Terrell had seen about recently. She had long flaxen hair and not a shred of clothing upon her. Master Richards, a short wiry man, had on his trousers and shirt.

"Ladies and gentlemen," greeted Master Richards, "thank you for joining me this evening. I would like to introduce you to my new submissive one, Miss Lily."

"Very lovely," remarked a woman in the audience.

"Say thank you, Miss Lily."

"Thank you," said Miss Lily in a small voice. She kept her hands folded demurely before her and her eyes downcast.

Master Richards turned back to the audience. "Miss Lily is displayed tonight for your enjoyment. What do you wish I should do with her?"

His question elicited a variety of responses.

"Flog her."

"Cane her."

"Make her crawl at your feet."

"Tie her up."

The last suggestion captured his interest. He turned to someone in the front row. "We might be in luck tonight, for we have amongst us a Master most talented in the art of rope bondage. Master Gallant, would you do us the honor of demonstrating your skills?"

Terrell started. Master Gallant was still here?

"Pray, honor us," someone in the audience said.

"Yes, please," said another.

Master Gallant rose to his feet and stepped onto the stage. Master Richards handed him a cord of rope, which Gallant tested as he unfurled it. He glanced at Miss Lily, who had drawn in a sharp breath but looked quite pleased with the turn of affairs.

Terrell felt the stirrings of jealousy. She would have liked to be bound in rope by Master Gallant in front of an audience. She studied Miss Lily, young and fair, with pretty golden curls at her mons. No doubt they were soft and silky to the touch. The lucky wench.

Behind Miss Lily, a long wooden beam stretched between two racks. Master Gallant looked between Miss Lily and the beam.

"Hands behind your back," he instructed Miss Lily.

He bound her wrists behind her, then called for another cord of rope. The second one he wrapped above her breasts, then below her breasts, and draped the rope around her rib cage as if it were a garland of adornment. Murmurs of approval swept through the audience.

Terrell felt her pulse quicken. Miss Lily looked lovely decorated with rope. Though Terrell sat farthest from the stage, she could see Miss Lily's breath becoming more and more uneven each time Master Gallant's hand grazed her body. Terrell wondered if Gallant could be aroused by the petite form of Miss Lily, but she could not see his crotch from where she sat.

With a third and lengthy cord of rope, Gallant bound Miss Lily's ankles together.

"Lie down," he told her.

With his aid, Miss Lily laid herself upon the stage.

"I fear the members sitting in the back will not be able to see her," Richards said.

"They will," Gallant replied.

He tested the sturdiness of the wood beam, tossed the end of the rope over it, and, with the rope, pulled Miss Lily's ankles into the air. A woman in the audience gasped. After securing the rope, Gallant stood aside. Miss Lily hung with her legs in the air, but the beam was not high enough to suspend all of her. Thus, the topmost part of her body, from her head to the midpoint of her sides, still reclined upon the stage.

"Stupendous," Richards praised. He put a booted foot upon the side of Miss Lily's head. "Did you thank Master Gallant?"

She obeyed. "Thank you, Master Gallant."

Richards inserted a finger between her thighs and withdrew it glistening with moisture. "I believe she is partial to your bondage, Master Gallant. Perhaps you would care to make the first strike tonight?"

Richards presented Gallant the flogger. Terrell shifted in her seat and tried to stay her jealousy. Of course he would accept. Miss Lily, though young, was undoubtedly more his preference, with her pale skin and innocent features.

"Thank you," Gallant replied. "But I am done for the evening."

Terrell sighed in relief as Gallant returned to his seat.

"Master Troy, you have a masterful hand with the flogger," Richards offered.

A brawny man rose from his seat and stepped onto the stage. He took the flogger and was about to whip it against her legs when Gallant interrupted.

"Has Miss Lily a safety word?"

"Of course," Richards answered. "She had requested the word 'rose' and I agreed to it."

"Master Troy must know it, too."

Realizing his omission, Richards turned to the man nearly double his size. "Rose."

Master Troy nodded, then landed the flogger upon Miss Lily. She screamed. Surprisingly loud for someone with such a slight frame, Terrell thought. She remembered when the flogger with knots had slashed her already torn and bloodied back. The pain of it was so great, it had rendered her screams silent.

Miss Lily continued to scream as the tails landed upon her thighs and arse. Though Terrell found her high-pitched wails grating on the ears, she could not deny that the sight of her—slender legs stretched above her, her hair tangled upon the stage, her pert nipples pointed downward—was quite provocative. Terrell pressed her thighs together. Heat stirred in her groin as she wondered what other manner of bondage Master Gallant could contrive? How might he bend or twist the supple female form into submission?

"Thank you," Miss Lily whispered when Master Troy had finished.

"What more shall we submit the lovely Miss Lily to?" Richards asked of the audience.

"Adorn her nipples with clamps," offered one member. "She has charming little teats."

"That she has," agreed Richards. He went to a small table and selected two clamps, each with weights attached to them.

Miss Lily emitted a piercing cry when Richards fixed the first clamp to her nipple.

"Any more desires?" Richards asked after applying the second clamp. The implements pulled the nipples down toward the floor.

"Paddle her a whore," suggested Sophia.

Richards smiled and bowed. "I should be only too happy to oblige the beautiful Miss Sophia."

From the table he retrieved a wooden paddle with the word "whore" etched into it. He turned Miss Lily about so that her arse faced the audience.

"Would Miss Sophia care to honor me?" he inquired of her.

Sophia sauntered with swaying hips onto the stage. She received the paddle from Richards and held onto the handle as if wielding a cricket bat. Miss Lily howled at the first blow.

"Her safety word is 'rose'," Gallant reminded.

"Yes, Master Gallant," Sophia replied.

Over and over, Sophia struck at a buttock till the cheek blushed crimson. The word "whore" was faintly visible upon her flesh.

When Sophia was done, she turned to Master Gallant. "Do you approve, Master?"

Terrell stiffened, for the interest was plain upon Sophia's face.

"You had best direct the question to Master Richards," Gallant replied.

"Her workmanship is, without question, praiseworthy," Richards hastened to say. He took Sophia's hand and planted a kiss upon it.

But Sophia had only eyes for Gallant as she sat down. Terrell tried not to mind. Sofia was far from her favorite at the Red Chrysanthemum.

Richards returned to Miss Lily. "My dear, you have done well. Now you shall be rewarded for your efforts. How do you wish to be pleasured?"

Miss Lily answered in a quiet voice. Richards had to bend down to hear. When he straightened, he looked to

Gallant.

"Master Gallant, may I ask a favor? Will you indulge my submissive one and grant her wish?"

Terrell drew in a sharp breath. Though she knew she had no claim upon him, she did not think she could bear to watch Master Gallant sink his cock into a cunnie not her own. Perhaps she ought to leave.

And yet she could not. A strange pairing of jealousy and arousal stayed her.

She watched as Master Gallant stepped onto the stage, taking some consolation in the lack of eagerness upon his countenance. He surveyed Miss Lily before turning her to face the audience.

"Have you ever had others bear witness to you in divine paroxysm?" he asked Miss Lily.

"No, Master Gallant."

"Then tonight will be your first. These men and women will watch as your body succumbs to carnal pleasure. Their gaze will feast upon you. Your arousal will stir their arousal, and your pleasure will be their pleasure."

He slid a hand between her thighs. She immediately moaned. He stroked her, eliciting all manner of groans and gasps.

Damn. Damn. Damn, Terrell cursed. Desire blossomed in her groin even as her chest constricted at the sight of his hand upon another woman.

"You may spend whenever you wish, Miss Lily."

Terrell gaped and could not refrain herself from voicing, "Are you always so quick and ready with the granting of permissions?"

Everyone turned in her direction.

"Miss Lily has proven herself to be a well-behaved submissive," Gallant replied without emotion.

"As docile as a kitten," Richards added.

Terrell said nothing more, and all attention was returned to the stage.

Well-behaved. Docile. These were qualities Gallant would not ascribe to her. Terrell looked down. Would she ever meet his satisfaction? Even if she tried her best, how could she compare to the likes of Miss Lily?

Terrell stared at the legs of the chair before her. No doubt Gallant considered her a saucy and unruly blackamoor. Perhaps he would have taken her for his submissive if she were more like Miss Lily.

"Do you see the effect you have?" Gallant asked of Miss Lily.

Richards had pulled out his cock and was vigorously stroking himself. Another member had his submissive upon his lap as he caressed her breasts. She arched into him. Beside them, a woman had her hand up the skirts of her Mistress.

"Y-Yes," Miss Lily replied, her body twitching. "Oh! I am to spend, Master! Master!"

Her body convulsed. With a grunt, Richards came to his climax and spewed his seed upon Miss Lily. It struck her belly and slid toward her breasts. She shivered and gasped as Gallant gently coaxed the last of her paroxysms from her.

Terrell bit her bottom lip. She was filled with envy. She wanted to be there upon the stage with Master Gallant. She would have done whatever he wished to prove she could be as good a submissive as Miss Lily.

"Lower the rope and release her bonds," Gallant instructed Richards before the latter could collapse into a nearby chair.

With a nod, Richards did as commanded. Gallant

returned to his seat as the audience quietly applauded.

"If you would be so gracious as to impart some of your skills with the ropes," Richards said to Gallant, "I would gift you the lovely Miss Lily—with Madame's approval, of course."

Terrell gripped the edge of her chair. Who would refuse such a gift? Among the younger women, only Sophia could be deemed prettier. But the latter had none of Miss Lily's innocence, which made her seem barely a day older than six and ten.

"My approval is not required," Madame Devereux replied as she stood, turning to the members. "It is entirely up to Master Gallant, for he is to take my place for the sennight. I am to be absent and, during that time, he will run the Red Chrysanthemum in my stead. He has full authority to undertake whatever he desires and to approve or revoke any membership as he sees fit. He will be the sole proprietor of the inn, and my staff will serve at his pleasure. I depart in the morning but could not leave the inn in more capable hands."

A quiet murmur followed her announcement.

"Master Gallant, you honor us," Richards said with a bow.

"How kind of you to undertake such a responsibility," Sophia said. "Know that you may avail yourself of my *assistance* in *anything* you may require. I should be happy to serve at your pleasure."

Other members began to crowd about him and Madame. Terrell, however, kept her distance. Her pulse had quickened at this most surprising turn of events. She would have Master Gallant for a sennight! If he was assuming Madame's role, he would have to come to the inn every night.

But with the full authority Madame described, he could do as he wished. He could choose any member for his own. Miss Lily. Miss Sophia. Even Mistress Scarlet if she were here. Or all three of them.

The thought made Terrell ill. She had never felt such jealousy before. The dreadful feeling came upon her sudden and strong. Not knowing what to make of it, she made her way out the room. In the hallway, she came across Sarah.

"Have I missed the announcement?" Sarah asked.

"May I make use of your shawl?" Terrell asked.

"You may, but why? What is it?"

"I mean to take a stroll."

"At this hour?"

"I shall not stray far."

"What did Madame Devereux say?"

"She is to be gone a sennight, and Master Gallant will govern the inn in her absence."

"Indeed?"

Terrell didn't stay to answer any more questions and, throwing the borrowed shawl about her shoulders, whisked by Baxter and out the front door. She hurried down the front steps and into the coolness of night.

The moon, near full and between clouds, cast its white light upon the cobbled street. She walked at a brisk pace past vacant shops, including one that was once a bookstore and another that was a printing establishment, as if she could distance herself from the tightness that gripped her. She had told Sarah she intended a stroll, but, in truth, she merely wanted to be away from *him,* from the sight of Sophia fawning over him.

Her stomach twisted as if she had partaken of spoiled meat. This sensation had a distressing hold of her. From where did it spring? She had never before experienced this manner of unease. She was not unfamiliar with jealousy. She had felt its pangs in Barbados when witnessing Creoles clothed as elegantly as white women, when she suffered their condescension. Though they had not the status of white women, Terrell found herself more jealous of the former. When she had become a courtesan in her own right, she could have rivaled any of the finely dressed Creoles.

The ache overcoming her now, however, had a depth she found bewildering. When would it pass? Or would it only worsen? She ought to be overjoyed at the prospect of Master Gallant at the Red Chrysanthemum every night for a sennight. But could she bear to watch Sophia batting her lashes at him? Could he be swayed by Sophia? Or the charming blush of Miss Lily? Would he avail himself of one of them? She shuddered at the prospect. What was she to do? How could she rid herself of the dreadful wrenching inside of her?

She stumbled when her foot struck an upturned stone, but righted herself and continued on her way. What ailed her? She was not herself. What should it matter whom Sophia attempted to seduce? What should it matter if Master Gallant should choose the likes of Sophia or Miss Lily for his own? A man as delicious as Master Gallant ought be shared.

But she wanted him all to herself. All of him. If he should take another, the withering pain, its roots already sunken into her belly, would be too great.

"Miss Terrell!"

She recognized the voice behind her but pretended not to hear. She needed time and solitude to tame the swirl of emotions sweeping through her.

"Terrell!"

The footsteps behind her quickened.

"Stop!"

He had barked the command with as much displeasure as she had ever heard from Master Gallant.

She stopped.

He drew up before her, holding a lantern, his countenance stern, his jaw tight, his stare intense. She suddenly felt like a child who had committed a grievous wrong.

"It is beyond foolhardy for a woman to walk these streets alone," he said.

A part of her warmed at the thought that he had come out in search of her, but she was still nettled at him. He could have declined to pleasure Miss Lily, but he had not. Terrell wondered if he had accepted Master Richard's offer.

"I did not intend to walk far," she replied, though she had not given her stroll much forethought.

A vein in his neck pulsed. "And for what purpose do you seek a stroll at this hour?"

She affected a nonchalance that belied the turmoil inside. "It seemed as good an hour as any."

He looked at her as if she spoke madness. Straightening, he asked impassively, "Did you partake of a beverage as I had instructed you to?"

She hesitated too long to accomplish a lie. She squared her shoulders. "I intended to but was informed that Madame was to make an important announcement."

From his expression, she knew that he did not accept her defense.

"You will return to the inn now," he told her, "and imbibe—"

"I am not yet done with my stroll."

"You will find a more appropriate and safer time to take your stroll."

If she were a cat or dog, she would have growled at him. She had no desire to face him at present, not till she had these wretched emotions in hand. They weakened her. She suspected that, to gain mastery over them, she would have to relinquish her interest in Master Gallant. It would not matter then what he did with Miss Lily or Sophia or anyone.

"I am not yours to command," she said. To her surprise, her voice quivered as she spoke. She brushed by him before she was overcome.

In a few steps, he had caught her. Wrapping his arm about her waist, he pulled her to him. Her back slammed into his chest. He had set the lantern down, and his other hand was beneath her jaw, tilting her head up and to the side so that he could speak into her ear.

"That is easy enough to rectify, Miss Terrell."

Her heart raced. What did he mean by that statement?

"You may have Madame's authority," she managed, though it was not easy to speak when he had such a forceful grip upon her, "but even she does not dictate my—"

His hold upon her tightened. She did not attempt to struggle. She dared not even squirm.

"I am more than Madame to you," he said. "I am your Master."

Chapter Sixteen

I *am your master.*

The words echoed several times through her head.

"As my submissive, you will heed me at all times. Do you understand, Miss Terrell?"

She could hardly think. Was this truly happening?

He lifted her chin higher, but still she could barely see him from the corners of her eyes.

"I will not repeat myself, Miss Terrell."

Elation slowly seeped into her. "Yes, Master, I understand."

"Good."

He released her jaw, and she released the breath she had been holding. His other arm still held her to him, and her body could not resist responding to his nearness, which always overwhelmed all else.

His free hand slid down into her décolletage, forcing its way into her tight stays. She moaned at the feel of his hand over a breast. Her earlier arousal had not fully disappeared. It made its presence known with a flare of heat in her groin. His other hand dropped from her waist and cupped her mons through her skirts. Resistance was futile. She wondered that she could ever resist his touch. If he wanted to fuck her there in the streets, she would have allowed it.

Desired it even.

He seemed to know her thoughts and asked, "Did you

enjoy Miss Lily's performance?"

"Yes, Master," she answered, her breath catching when he rubbed her skirts between her legs. She should have donned another layer of petticoat for her wetness was sure to soil her dress.

"Were you aroused?"

"Yes, Master."

"Would you have liked to take her place?"

"Yes, especially when you were pleasuring her."

"I would have had you endure much before rewarding you."

Her legs weakened at the thought of being on stage with Master Gallant. "I would have relished it all, Master."

"Would you? What if I bid you wear naught but the shirt I gifted you?"

"I should be pleased to do as you bid."

"And pleasured yourself for all to see?"

"There would be no finer performance."

He grunted. She shifted her arse against him, searching for evidence of his arousal.

"Stay as you are, Miss Terrell," he warned. "Consider your body my instrument, to stroke and play as I wish."

It was as he described, and her body knew no music more beautiful than what he plied. She stilled herself, though she tensed when she heard a rustling sound. But it was more likely to be a rat than a person.

When all was quiet again, he asked, "What if I had you pleasure every member of the audience before you could spend?"

"I would suck as many cocks as you desired."

"And lick as many cunnies?"

"I think you have seen my talents with the fair sex."

He grunted once more. She tried not to writhe, but his

ministrations between her legs were wreaking havoc on her nerves. He squeezed her breast.

"How would you enjoy being paddled in the arse while you applied that delightful tongue of yours to Miss Lily?"

"I would enjoy it very much, Master."

"Or perhaps I would bend you over atop a table with your arse high in the air for the audience to behold, and all of them invited to spank it red with an implement of their choosing. Their hand, the paddle, crop, flogger, switch."

"Please do, Master," she said, though what she wanted to beg was for him to fondle her till she spent. The friction of the fabric against her clitoris was delightful, and she could feel herself at the edge.

"Please what?"

"P-Please present my arse for all to spank, Master. Please, Master."

"A good submissive knows not to spend lest permitted."

Her teeth chattered as he kept up the vigor of his rubbing She squeezed her eyes shut as she attempted to keep the tension from unfurling into ecstasy.

"You know this, Miss Terrell."

"Y-Yes." She pressed the back of her head into his chest to keep her body from shuddering. It seemed the torrent of her earlier emotions, as uncomfortable as they were, had lent their intensity to the pleasure building inside of her.

"Please, may I, Master?" she pleaded.

"May you?"

"Spend. Please."

By way of answer, he removed his hand from between her legs. Her nerves screamed at the deprivation of his touch. Her body hung upon a cliff, unable to fall into the rapture below and requiring some time before it could retreat back over the edge.

He kept his hand over her breast longer before withdrawing. Eyes shut, she took several breaths to calm the riot in her body. When she opened her eyes, she found herself in his gaze. He knew her body too well, knew precisely when to withdraw to produce the greatest agony, knew how to entice it to its doom. She cursed him silently.

"Tomorrow we begin your discipline, Miss Terrell. You are in want of much disciplining. You will be tempted to pleasure yourself to spend tonight, but you will never spend without first obtaining my permission. Disobey once and your submission to me is at an end. Do you understand, Miss Terrell?"

"Yes, Master."

"When I return tomorrow evening, you will be provided instructions. You will obey them all without question, without hesitation, and with none of your waywardness or impudence."

"Yes, Master."

"Now return to the inn."

"Yes, Master."

Realizing he did not intend to touch her further, she reluctantly turned from him, arousal still humming in her loins, and headed back. He stood with arms crossed and watched her. When she reached the inn, she could see that he had not moved from his spot down the street. Picking up her skirts, she went up the steps. Baxter waited at the door with a glass of lemonade.

"Master Gallant said this was for you," he said.

Accepting the glass, she gulped its contents, hoping it would cool the ardor between her legs. She then made her way back to her room. Sarah was lying beside a softly snoring George. Upon Terrell's return, she rose from her bed.

"Did Master Gallant find you?" she asked as she assisted Terrell from her gown.

"He did."

"He seemed concerned for you."

"Did he?"

"Do not feign modesty with me, miss. You've done it. You've gone and seduced Master Gallant."

Terrell caught her breath. Had she? She supposed she had. It was a triumph that ought to have thrilled her. It *did* thrill her. But she found she was also a little petrified at the path she had chosen to descend.

Chapter Seventeen

Though not yet the Season, The Istanbul Coffee House still enjoyed ample business in the mornings, its long wooden tables more than half filled with patrons. At one table, a man stood reading poetry to anyone who would listen. At another table, two men compared the merits of Jamaican coffee to Turkish coffee. The page, an Indian boy, hustled about the room refilling cups and collecting the occasional perquisite.

On his second cup of coffee, Charles endeavored his best to take in the complaints of Mr. Bartholomew Morton, who owned the fourth largest bank in London. Beside him sat Sir George Canning with the morning edition of *The Times,* engrossed by the news or using it as a convenient excuse to pay no heed to the banker.

"This coffee tastes of shit," Mr. Morton grumbled, setting down his cup. "The coffee at Jonathan's is much better. I should take myself there more often were The Istanbul not so conveniently situated. How fares the election, Charles?"

"I shall have a better answer for you in five weeks' time," Charles replied as he contemplated a third cup.

After conferring with Joan on the details of his interim governance of the inn, he had arrived home to find Wang, his valet, waiting for him. Wang never failed to greet him when he returned, no matter the hour. Though Charles was indebted to the Chinaman, without whom he would not have been able to travel outside the factory in Canton, Wang felt he owed Charles the greater debt for rescuing his younger brother from the wrath of the local governor, and arranging for the second son and his wife to find safety and employment in England.

Charles had stayed up late instructing Wang on the preparations needed for his stay at the Red Chrysanthemum. In truth, he had had little desire to sleep at the moment. *She* still occupied his body. He had left Miss Terrell aroused and wanting, but in doing so, he had imposed the same discontent upon himself. He could make himself spend, but it would not satisfy. His cock needed to be buried inside of her.

He had seen her sitting in the back row—indeed, he had looked for her presence as soon as he had stepped onto the stage—and had glimpsed the lust in her countenance as he pleasured Miss Lily. He had seen, too, her consternation as she quit the room. He knew not what caused it. Perhaps she had been jealous of Miss Lily. Strangely compelled to understand the nature of her displeasure, he had excused himself to the throng gathering about him and learned from Baxter which direction Miss Terrell had headed.

What followed had been unexpected. In the streets, surrounded by darkness but for the light of the moon, it felt as if he and Miss Terrell were engaged in a lovers' quarrel. He knew a part of him wanted desperately to tame the panther, discipline the unruly minx and assert his dominance with her. But he had not committed himself to being her Master till that moment.

Perhaps it was the authority of his new position, though he had not thought himself a man whom power could intoxicate. But he could not deny the thrill that came from conquering her with pleasure. He wanted to possess her, to have her all to himself, this dark beauty whom Sir Arthur wished to claim for his own. Charles had to admit to feeling a small, petty satisfaction where that gentleman was concerned.

"When you are MP," Mr. Morton said, "you will of course disregard this nonsense Sir Webb is seeking with regards to this West African Squadron."

"Do you not support abolition, Mr. Morton?" Charles asked.

Mr. Morton blustered. "Of course I do, but we are at war, sir. We cannot divert the precious resources of our Royal Navy to patrolling slave ships. Mark me, we underestimate Napoleon at our peril."

"Then for certain you will not wish to see Mr. Laurel elected," said Sir Canning, putting down the paper. "The man once expressed support for the Jacobins. And, having secured the support of Lady Holland, he has no small chance of winning."

"I thought Charles to have the support of Sir Arthur? Surely that is all that is needed."

"I will take nothing for granted, especially the support of Sir Arthur," replied Charles, tipping the page after receiving his third cup of coffee.

"And Sir Arthur is away at the moment," Sir Canning added. "I am certain he will grant Charles his full backing when he returns, if modesty would permit Charles to request it."

Charles drank his coffee. It was not modesty that stalled him.

"You may count upon my support," Mr. Morton said, "especially if you have the endorsement of Sir Arthur. He is an extraordinary gentleman. I daresay his star would rise as high as any but for that sad business that hangs like the shadow of rainclouds. Perhaps it will dissipate in time."

"What 'sad business'?" Charles asked, now very awake.

"Do you not know?"

"I was in the Orient for two years."

"Ah, yes, it was sad business. Sad business indeed."

"Do you allude to the passing of his wife?"

"Sir Arthur was exonerated," said Sir Canning. "It was a tragic accident that took the life of his wife."

"Thank God the doctor saved the babe or Arthur would have lost wife and child. It is sad enough for a man to lose his wife, but to have the indignity of an inquiry and accusations of foul play…"

"When a man is as influential and revered as Sir Arthur, he cannot exist without enemies."

"What was the nature of the accident?" Charles persisted. "How was the babe at risk?"

"Sir Arthur's wife was with child when she fell down the stairs and broke her neck."

"And it would have been a simple tragedy were it not for the hysterics of a maid given to delusions," said Sir Canning.

"The wench claimed Sir Arthur had deliberately pushed his wife down the stairs."

Charles felt the hairs on his neck stand. He would not have discounted the maid so easily.

"Made quite the hullabaloo and the wife's family believed her," said Mr. Morton. He tried his coffee a second time, made a face, and set the cup back down.

"But no worthy magistrate would take the word of a silly maid over that of a distinguished gentlemen," Sir Canning said.

"Sir Arthur, good man that he was, despite her

attempts to smear his good name, had even offered to find her new employment, for apparently she was a devoted maid of his wife's. I should have left the girl to fend for herself without any references."

A young man approached their table. "Mr. Gallant, is it true you have the backing of Sir Arthur, and that he will turn out of doors any resident who does not vote for you? You must approve of such tactics if you've accepted his support."

Sir Canning narrowed his eyes. "I know you. You're Mr. Phillips with *The Independent*, an Opposition paper."

"Sir, I am but a humble journalist seeking to write the truth of what transpires. A democracy without transparency is no democracy."

Mr. Morton snorted. "And who wishes for democracy? Not I."

Charles rose to his feet. "I do *not* condone coercion, Mr. Phillips, or corruption of our electoral system."

"If I may, Mr. Gallant, you sound akin to a Foxite," the young man said, scribbling away upon his pad of paper.

"He is not a Foxite. He is merely a man of integrity," Sir Canning said. "Now be off with you."

"I have but a few more questions for Mr. Gallant."

"Alas, I must beg my leave," said Charles. "I have several hours of campaigning ahead of me and many voters to talk to."

"Talk to voters?" Morton chortled. "Why talk when you can simply ply them with drink? There's democracy for you, Mr. Phillips."

The banker laughed heartily. Charles bid the men good day and took his leave of the coffeehouse, but Mr. Phillips trailed after him.

"I understand the Brentwoods have not yet announced

whom they are supporting," said Mr. Phillips. "You seem the likely candidate. Why have they not publicly announced their backing?"

"Had you better not ask the Brentwoods?" Charles returned. "I can only provide you speculation, and, as a capable journalist, you would not substitute hearsay for fact."

"Sir Canning spoke of integrity, and from what I can find, you have no blemishes upon your reputation. None that are known, that is. Your family is well respected. But would you say that no man is perfect? We all have hidden blemishes."

"What does Mr. Laurel say?"

"I have not posed the question to him."

"Then do me this favor, Mr. Phillips: prove to me that your paper can print an unbiased article and I will gladly answer all your questions. Good day, Mr. Phillips."

Charles was relieved when the journalist did not follow. *The Independent* was known for digging up scandals it could attach to Tories. If his patronage of the Red Chrysanthemum should be known to the likes of Mr. Phillips, it might prove disastrous to his election, if not his career. But he had agreed to assist Joan in her time of need, and he would not shirk the responsibility.

Nevertheless, it was clear that spending a sennight at the Red Chrysanthemum was a risky proposition.

Chapter Eighteen

The woman who could make all the difference for Charles sat across from him in the well-appointed drawing room, her posture impeccable, making her seem quite tall though she remained seated. Mrs. Mathilda Brentwood had a narrow physiognomy and, unlike most women her age, wore little in the way of powder or other cosmetics to disguise the wrinkles and blemishes. She poured a cup of tea and handed it to Charles.

"My apologies for the tardiness of a reply," Mrs. Brentwood began. "My husband and I are normally quite engaged in the elections, but we have been away from town because we had a pressing family matter to attend to."

"I pray it has been resolved to your satisfaction," Charles ventured, having heard rumors that Mrs. Brentwood's niece had run off to Gretna Green with a young man the family did not approve of.

"It has. My niece was married a fortnight ago by a special license my husband's cousin was able to procure. She is now Mrs. Cornwall."

Mrs. Brentwood sniffed, conveying that she took little pleasure in the name she had just uttered.

"Many happy returns," Charles said nevertheless.

"Yes, well, now that she and young Cornwall are settled, my husband having secured a good placement for him, I can turn my attention to Porter's Hill. Our families are a little acquainted. Regretfully, we could not support your father in the last election, but that will have no bearing upon your standing. I have heard naught but good of you and your service to Sir Canning," Mrs. Brentwood continued, "and that you are likely to receive the endorsement of Sir Arthur. If that is so, our support is unnecessary."

"I would not discount the value of your support, and I should be honored to have it. Sir Arthur does not own a majority of the borough and is out of town at the moment."

"That Mr. Laurel is still the only Whig in the race?"

"He is."

"Hm. I do not fear that one more Whig will affect our stronghold in Parliament, but we ought not give them any encouragement, not when so much is at stake for England and her interests. I have little doubt you will make a fine Member of Parliament, Mr. Gallant."

"I certainly shall endeavor not to disappoint."

"I should like nothing more than to support your candidacy, Mr. Gallant."

Charles sat at attention, sensing disappointment in her demeanor.

"But I must be candid," she said, "and I hope you will not think less of me for it."

"I welcome your candor and bid you speak freely."

"My brother owns a sugar plantation in Jamaica. They have been hard hit these past years. With the war on the Continent, an entire market has been lost to us. Last year, sugar from Jamaica sold at less than the cost to produce it. My brother says they talk of nothing but debt, disease and death. Amidst all this, the Abolition Committee wishes to deprive planters of their primary source of labor?"

Charles set down his cup and saucer. "I am sorry to hear of the tribulations facing your family. If I may impose upon your candor, Mrs. Brentwood, are you opposed to abolition?"

"No. I am not opposed to abolition. I applaud Sir Wilberforce and his accomplishment. Though my brother was concerned for how the end of the slave trade would affect him, he has enough healthy, young slaves at present and expects he can purchase more from the Americans if needed. I am told tobacco does not tire the slaves as much as the harvesting of sugar. But the complete abolition of slavery throughout the entire empire would doom my brother. Lest prices improve, the business of sugar is unsustainable without slaves."

"Do you mean to say your brother is opposed to abolition?"

"His situation forces his hand on the matter."

"And you must find yourself in an awkward place to have to disagree with him."

"Yes, well, I support abolition, but I do not see the necessity to rush into it."

"I think those opposed to slavery settled on putting an end to the trade of slaves because they knew they could not be successful in more than that."

"Nevertheless, they were quite buoyed by their success in abolishing the slave trade. They will not rest until every last slave is free."

"And you worry that I favor abolition?"

"In truth, you may support it or not. I wish to see good men elected. Men who can lead England through a trying time and see to the defeat of France. My only request on the matter of abolition is that you not favor it at this time. What harm could come of it if we were to wait ten or fifteen years?"

"Ten or fifteen years could be a lifetime for a slave."

"But plantation owners must be given time to prepare and adjust to such drastic changes. We would put them all out of business with a stroke of the pen."

"And with one stroke of the pen, thousands would know the greatest joy and have that which surely every Englishman would not live without: freedom."

"I see where your principles lie, but surely you do not wish to crumble a most important segment of our economy. What would happen to our interests in the West Indies? I daresay every Englishman needs fear for his life if we were to free the slaves. Such an undertaking must be done *methodically*, with care and measure given to the safety and wellbeing of His Majesty's citizens."

"What of the safety and wellbeing of the slaves? They lead not pretty lives." In his mind flashed the image of Miss Terrell's scarred back. "They lead a gruesome existence. Do we not have a responsibility to care for them, especially as they did not choose their circumstances?"

"I agree with you, Mr. Gallant, and I support any rule that would make it a crime to mistreat slaves. That may tide us over till we are in a better position to consider any sweeping declarations of abolition."

Charles said nothing. He would have voted in favor of an abolition bill.

"I, too, wish to see abolition become law," said Mrs. Brentwood. "I only wish to urge caution and *patience*. I would do so even if my family had no interest in the matter."

"And your support of my candidacy rests upon my patience?"

"I believe you more qualified for the burgess than Mr. Chester and hope you can accommodate my request. It is not without merit. There are many considerations that Parliament must undertake. We need not rush to place abolition before all other worthy matters of weight."

"Your support is contingent upon this?"

"I fear it is."

"And you would favor Mr. Chester if I am unable to agree?"

"If you have the support of Sir Arthur, my support of Mr. Chester will not matter."

Charles did not dispute her, but he had hoped not to require the support of Sir Arthur. While Sir Arthur may not concern himself much on the matter of slavery, he would expect Charles to fall in line on matters that did compel him. Charles would rather not serve in Parliament at all than serve as that man's puppet.

Chapter Nineteen

Sarah had taken George downstairs to look for bread crust that the boy could gnaw upon, leaving Terrell alone in their chambers, waiting for instructions from Master Gallant. She wished the window of their room faced the street, that she might see his arrival. Instead, their room faced the building behind.

She had struggled with what to wear. The pale blue muslin was her best gown, but she had worn it yesterday. Though she had little to choose from, decision evaded her for some time. She finally settled upon the attire she was most comfortable with: a corset worn over her shift, a calf-length skirt and petticoats. She did not understand why she should feel nervous. Had she not wanted this, to be Master Gallant's submissive? Had she not craved for him to claim her?

Yes and yes. She could hardly believe her luck. And, to think, but last night she had nearly given up hope of such a thing, had thought she might need relinquish her desire for him. Why he had a change of mind, she did not know. And she supposed he was likely to change his mind yet again. He would have awakened this morning and remembered the reasons why he had resisted her before. Master Gallant did not appear a capricious man, but even the most stalwart succumbed to errors in judgment.

A knock at the door startled her. Was it Master Gallant? Had he sent one of the servants to collect her?

She opened the door to find an Oriental man whom she had never before seen. She had only ever seen one of his kind from afar. His hair was as black as hers. It was cropped short but did not appear at all to curl as her locks did. His eyes, shaped entirely different from any she knew, were also darker than hers and possessed an unsettling intensity, as if taking in every detail all at once. His expression, at rest, was stern.

"Come," he said.

Terrell would have balked at such orders coming from a stranger, but this man spoke with such calm confidence, she felt both compelled and comforted at the same time. When he turned and proceeded down the hall, she followed.

Remembering that Gallant had spent years in the Orient, she asked, "Did Master Gallant send you?"

"Yes."

His curt tone indicated he was not a man of conversation. He led her to a small but separate wing of the inn. Only Madame occupied this wing.

"Are you his servant?" Terrell guessed when he opened the door to Madame's chambers.

"His valet."

Terrell was familiar with the antechamber, but she had never before entered the bedroom. The Oriental opened the door to the inner room. The sight of it stunned Terrell.

Her owner in Barbados had a chamber as ornate—no, more elaborate—than the one she stood in, but the starkness of the rest of the inn made Madame's chambers opulent in comparison. The large four-post bed with valance and thick drapes was fit for a king. A fire crackled beneath a marble mantle and large looking glass. Silk wallpaper and golden candelabras adorned the walls. The polished furnishings, all in the Chippendale style, added more luxury to the surroundings. Only the paintings of naked nymphs and men sporting wakened cocks, an ivory handled cane, a jeweled flogger, and a cage gave evidence that this was no ordinary bedchamber.

"Sit," the Oriental said, indicating a chair before a small table set with tea.

She did as he bid and watched him pour a cup of tea. "Is Master Gallant here?"

He handed her the cup of tea. "Drink."

The tea smelled fragrant, but it was not one she had tried before. She took a sip and could not decide if she favored the unfamiliar flavors. The tea had hints of fruit but also a slight bitterness.

"Drink."

She eyed the solemn man and began to wonder if it was wise to take his direction without question.

"The tea enhances stamina and improves health," he explained.

As it sounded of something Gallant would recommend, she took another sip. It was merely tea. What harm could it inflict?

"Drink all."

Standing before her, he crossed his arms as if he would not budge till she had finished.

"Will you drink any or will you merely watch me drink?" she asked, arching a brow, testing this impassive man. He was shorter than the average man, but she suspected his smaller build disguised a concentrated strength.

He did not answer.

"When do you expect Master Gallant?" she tried again between sips of the tea.

Still no answer.

"Have you any biscuits? I feel hungry of a sudden."

The man looked unamused. "Drink the tea."

Disappointed, she decided to finish the tea in a few gulps. She set the cup down. "Is that to your satisfaction?"

Ignoring her question, he said, "Undress."

She blinked several times. Who was this taciturn Oriental? She draped herself over the arm of her chair and raised a brow. "It is common to have an agreed-upon price for such a privilege."

The man remained impervious. "Master Gallant gave strict orders to return you to your room if you disobey."

A shiver went through her. Perhaps it was the choice in words. Disobey. Or the man's accent that made the word sound a little ominous.

She sat at attention. "May I have another cup of tea first?"

She took his lack of response as an assent. She poured herself a cup as she contemplated the situation. The man was Master Gallant's valet. It would not be out of order for Master Gallant to use the Oriental to carry out his directives. But why his valet?

Because Master Gallant could not send her written instructions.

"Have you served in Master Gallant's employ long?" she asked. When he made no answer, she asked, "Were you forbidden to speak to me?"

Still no answer. With a sigh, she finished her tea before setting the cup down. She stood up and faced him. "Undress, eh? That is an order from Master Gallant?"

"Yes."

"Now? Here?"

"Yes."

She smirked. "How lucky for you."

She supposed she had best obey and stepped away from the chair and tea table. First, she undid the pins and strings of her skirts and petticoats. Falling, they pooled at her feet. She looked the valet square in the face. He remained stoic, and she could detect no reaction. Was he a molly? She had never before come across a man who did not start at the prospect of a naked woman. She took the ribbons of her corset—a rare find, for it laced in front—and pulled the bow out. She loosened the ribbon grommet by grommet, then pushed the garment down her body to join the skirts already upon the floor. Standing in only her shift, she tossed her hair back.

"Satisfied?" she inquired, and thought she detected the first signs of his lust.

"Finish," he commanded, his gaze scanning her shift.

Slowly, she pushed the one sleeve then the other down her shoulders. She tugged the garment down. It slid past her beasts to her waist, then past the navel, hips and thighs on its descent to the floor. She now stood without a shred of clothing before the Oriental. It was hardly the first time she had stood naked before a man she had never before met, but his lack of expression, save for a slight upward tilt of the chin as he took in the sight of her, unnerved her a little.

She told herself that she was undressing for Master Gallant, that the eyes of the Oriental were proxies for the eyes of his employer. The thought titillated. Though a vibrant fire warmed the room, her nipples hardened.

She watched him place a handkerchief upon the armchair she had occupied earlier. It was a gilded French empire chair with an ample seat and fluted arms finished with scroll tops.

"Sit," he directed.

She obeyed. Against her bare bum, the silk handkerchief felt extravagant.

"Arouse yourself."

She took in a sharp breath before asking, "How do you want I should arouse myself?"

He took her hand and guided it to her mound, then resumed his detached stance. He would make an upstanding soldier, she decided as she swirled her fingers in the curls at her pelvis. He watched with what appeared to be a gleam in his eyes. She glanced at his crotch and hid her grin. He was not as impervious as she had first thought.

"It is quite wicked of Master Gallant to make me fondle myself before his valet," she murmured, sliding two fingers down to her folds. She lowered her lashes and imagined that he stood in the room with them, watching her. Feeling more relaxed, she rested her back against the chair and parted her thighs. Finding her clit, her fingers rubbed and pinched the bud, coaxing it to swell.

With a soft sigh, she frigged herself in earnest. Perhaps she could spend. She had spent the good part of the day thinking of Master Gallant, her body yearning to spend. For nearly four and twenty hours, she had been on edge. Several times she had considered touching herself. How easy it would have been, how tempting, to cast herself into that pool of ecstasy.

But Master Gallant had forbid it. And though he could not know for certain what she had or had not done, she felt he would. He would ask and know if she spoke false. She found she did not wish to lie to him. She wanted to make him proud.

Thus, she had refrained from even the simplest of

caresses for fear she would ignite a desire that she could not suppress. But it had been hard. So very hard. When her every thought turned to him, when the memories of his touch taunted, the deprivation of food and drink would have been easier to bear.

Having suffered the day without tending to, her body exalted in the current strokes. Moisture seeped from her folds and she rubbed it upon her clit, moaning as her digits quickened their glide. She had not realized the valet had moved till she sensed him standing before her. She hoped he did not mean to stop her.

He opened the small box he held. Nestled in the silk interior were two silver balls. He took her hand and set it upon the arm of the chair. Picking up one of the balls, he brushed it along her cunnie. She jumped at the coolness of the ball. She watched as he swirled the ball in her dampness, wondering how his fingers would feel upon her most sensitive parts. She wanted Master Gallant above all, but if he was not to come tonight, her heightened lust would settle for the touch of any member of his sex.

Coated, the ball was pushed between her folds till it disappeared inside her. She gasped, but her heat quickly warmed the sphere. Was it her imagination or had the ball vibrated somehow? She contemplated the sensation of the small weight resting inside her. It was not unpleasant, and she relished the feel of something in her cunnie.

He brushed the second ball along her slit. His finger grazed her flesh as he inserted the twin. It bumped into the first ball. She bit back a surprised oath. The balls *did* vibrate, or something akin to it. She had felt their tremor for a brief moment before they lay still once more. The Oriental replaced her hand.

"Continue," he said.

She stroked herself gently, her mind fixed upon the balls. She clenched her hungry cunnie down upon them. Their slight movement sent shivers of pleasure through her. What delightful objects! She fondled herself harder.

"Enough."

Groaning her reluctance, she withdrew her hand.

"Come."

She followed him. The balls, rolling inside her, wreaked havoc. She had to tighten her cunnie to keep them from slipping, yet they still managed to feel as if they were rolling to and fro, making her weak in the legs.

He stopped in front of the…cage. *Damn.*

She had been in cages before, cages far less comfortable than the one presented. Once, with Miss Isabelle, she had been cramped into a cage barely large enough to fit one person. Miss Isabelle, on the bottom, had to keep her knees bent and her head craned forward. Terrell, on top, straddled Isabelle with bent legs, her cunnie resting upon Isabelle's mouth. The two women had to lick each other. The first one to succeed in making the other spend would receive her freedom.

"Inside," the valet directed after he had opened the top of the cage.

Terrell climbed inside. The cage was not quite tall enough for her to be on her knees, but it was wide enough for her sit with her legs stretched in front of her.

He closed the top of the cage over her head and secured the lock. She hoped Master Gallant would arrive soon. Her body was on edge, and the balls rollicking inside her cunnie were driving her to madness.

"May I touch myself?" she asked.

The valet had walked away and went to collect the tea tray. "No."

She pursed her lips. "Will Master Gallant be here soon?"

"Perhaps."

He opened the door and left the room. Alone, she emitted a sigh of aggravation. He had finally answered a question of hers, and the answer was as vexing as none.

Her clit cried for attention, and she defiantly rubbed the desperate nub. But she would not spend. She would prove herself capable of obeying Master Gallant. Retracting her hand, she decided to lay upon her back with her knees bent. The Oriental had not said she could not pleasure herself at all. She lifted her hips and felt the delicious movement of the balls. She shivered. She lowered her hips. Best not to do too much or she would find herself spending.

As the cage had only vertical bars, it felt more spacious. She wondered if Madame always kept a cage in her chambers or if Master Gallant had brought it in. Looking up through the bars, she studied the paintings upon the ceiling. Naked cherubs framed couples in various positions of fornication: a man atop a woman, a woman atop a man, a man inserting his cock into the arse of another man, two women with lips locked and breasts touching. Terrell felt the heat in her groin deepen.

Her gaze shifted to the framed paintings upon the walls. In one of the paintings a satyr was ravishing a reluctant nymph. In another, the goddess Aphrodite had a cock in her mouth and in each hand. A third painting depicted the goddess Athena, clothed in armor but for her full and bare breasts, standing over several male warriors as they lay upon the ground, their cocks stiff in the air.

Her hand slid toward her mons, but she quickly snapped her hand away when the door opened. It was the valet.

She watched him as he went about his duties. He unpacked items from a portmanteau.

"Will Master Gallant be residing here?" she asked, then wondered why she bothered for she would receive no response.

She took to studying the Oriental, wondering at the length of his cock. He had a sinewy form. How might he appear naked? Despite his stoicism—he might be harder to seduce than even Master Gallant—how long would he last buried inside her cunnie? She squeezed the balls inside of her. If Master Gallant did not intend to fuck her tonight, she would gladly take his valet while he watched. She needed cock. Desperately.

And as if in answer to her prayers, she heard the tread of footsteps. They stopped at the threshold.

It was Master Gallant.

Chapter Twenty

G ood evening, Master Gallant," greeted Baxter with a touch more servility than he had evinced the evening before.

Charles handed the man his coat and hat. "I am the same man I was last night, Baxter."

"Yes, Master Gallant, and as always, if you should require anything of me, you have but to ask."

"Are there members here already?" Charles asked as he removed his gloves. He had hoped to arrive earlier, but he had agreed to a show at the Drury Theatre with the Dempseys. Mrs. Dempsey had taken a keen interest in Charles' election and promised to introduce him to several families whom she thought would be only too happy to support him. She had left the theater box several times to go in search of these acquaintances, conveniently leaving him alone with Miss Bridget Dempsey.

"Nicholas Edelton is here," Baxter replied. "And the new fellow who does nothing but watch them."

Charles wondered if it was the man whom Joan had dubbed her *voyeur*. "Where is the man? I have not had the pleasure of making his acquaintance."

"In the blue parlor. Would you care for me to bring you a drink, Master Gallant?"

"Your responsibility is to tend the door," Charles reminded him, "to ensure that only members are permitted inside."

"Yes, Master Gallant. As you wish, Master Gallant."

With a shake of the head, Charles headed for the blue parlor. He hoped not all the servants had turned into sycophants.

The *blue* of the parlor wallpaper and upholstery had long faded toward grey. The inn had a parlor decorated in the *chinoiserie* that was much nicer, but in his short time returned to the Red Chrysanthemum, he had noticed Mistress Primrose to favor the blue parlor despite her distinguished patrons.

Of mixed heritage, Mistress Primrose had a beauty more familiar to him, though parts of her reminded him of Miss Terrell. She had not quite the dramatic curves of the latter, but her form was plenty lovely. Charles could easily understand how so many members were taken by her. He had learned from Joan that Mistress Primrose was new to the ways of the Red Chrysanthemum and had learned under the tutelage of Mistress Scarlet.

Greta.

Greta would have made a fine instructor, despite her submissive nature. Charles waited for the pain to surface whenever he recalled Greta, but it was more of a wistful discomfort this night.

"Come, laugh at my little ugly duckling," Mistress Primrose urged two women who had been caressing each other upon a settee against the wall.

The two women obliged and walked over to where Nicholas Edelton—Charles believed his brother a marquess—knelt. Dressed in a woman's shift and stays, he had rouge smeared across his lips.

"She is indeed most homely," giggled one of the women.

"But most adept at cleaning slippers. Are you not, my pet?"

Charles crossed his arms before him. There was a bite to the woman's tone, as if she truly detested her submissive. He made a note to observe Mistress Primrose more in his time here. Joan had remarked that Nicholas Edelton, who was often accompanied by his cousin, would readily do anything for Mistress Primrose.

"He would make himself a eunuch for her," Joan had said.

And for some reason, Charles would not have been surprised if Mistress Primrose demanded just that. He turned his attention to where a man sat in the shadows behind a harpsichord. Wearing drab clothing, he had a stylus with which he would scratch words onto a small folded sheet of paper. Charles watched the man for several minutes before sauntering over and taking a seat beside him. The man quickly hid his paper and stylus.

"Good evening, Mr. Washington," Charles greeted.

"Good evening," the man grumbled, adjusting his hat as if he wished to conceal his countenance.

"George Washington, I'm told. A fine name. Fit for a president."

"Mr. Washington" grunted.

"Madame Devereux says you are here almost every night, but never engage in any of the activities."

"I like to watch."

"I can see. Is it Mr. Edelton or Mistress Primrose who has your attention?"

"Um, neither. I mean, I find them curious."

"Curious? You look damned uncomfortable."

The man shifted in his seat.

"Madame thinks you harmless," Charles continued,

"but I think otherwise, Mr. Washington. I know not your purpose, but it is plain you are not here to indulge in carnal pleasures. I wonder that you find anything here titillating?"

"Miss—er, Mistress Primrose. She is pretty."

"Only a blindman would say otherwise, but would I be wrong in suspecting that you have as much an interest in Mr. Edelton? He is a handsome young man."

Mr. Washington colored.

"There is no shame in finding our sex—"

"I am no molly, sir!"

His tone had the ring of sincerity to Charles. "Then what purpose does the Red Chrysanthemum serve for you, Mr. Washington? In truth, I see no reason why I should approve your continued patronage."

"Mistress Primrose. She…interests me."

"Earlier you disavowed any interest. I fully sanction the use of a *nom de plume*, shall we say, but no other forms of deceit. I must ask Jones to escort you—"

"But Madame has allowed my membership."

"And Madame has placed me in charge during her absence. I had not thought to invoke my full authority, but I will not risk the Red Chrysanthemum under my watch."

"Pray, good sir, I mean this establishment no harm."

Charles rose to his feet. "I fear I cannot trust that to be the case."

Mr. Washington also stood. "Wait! I… Is there a place we may speak in private?"

"Very well. If you will follow me, Mr. Washington."

Charles led the man to Madame's study and took a seat behind her writing table. Mr. Washington remained standing.

"I humbly request to be allowed to continue," he said.

"Much as I would like to, Mr. Washington—"

"Fields. My name is Fields."

Charles believed the man spoke true. "I appreciate your candor, Mr. Fields, but I find your attendance here suspect."

"I understand. You appear to me a man of integrity, and I hope that what I reveal to you will be kept in confidence?"

"Discretion is a pillar which the Red Chrysanthemum cannot exist without."

Mr. Fields removed his hat. "I have been tasked with following Mr. Nicholas Edelton."

"By whom?"

"By his family. They are concerned for him."

"I take it Mr. Edelton is unaware of your charge?"

"That is correct."

"I must say yours is a curious responsibility. Are you a relation of the Edelton family?"

"I am formerly with the Bow Street Runners. In my time as a Runner, I have been quite successful in tracking down the most elusive persons. I have recovered items of great value from crafty thieves, and, though I claimed no credit at the time, I helped discover the whereabouts of the Duchess of Hart."

"I remember Her Grace. She was living as a seamstress under an alias."

"For three years her family could not find her."

Charles studied the unassuming man. "You have a rare talent."

"I admit I enjoy the adventure."

"Can the Duke of Hart vouch for your efforts?"

"He can, but I prefer no accolades. I achieved my objective and was paid for my service. That is all I require."

For a moment, Charles, deep in thought, made no reply.

Taking the silence as hesitation, Mr. Fields added, "I assure you that I mean no harm to this establishment. My only task is to make an account of Mr. Edelton's activities."

"How can I trust that Mr. Edelton's family will not interfere with the affairs here? I doubt they would approve."

"As part of granting me access, Madame Devereux required I put down the requisite deposit, which I forfeit if any harm should come to the Red Chrysanthemum. I care not what transpires here."

"You must have an opinion."

"My opinion is irrelevant to my assignment, sir."

Satisfied, Charles leaned against the arm of his chair. "Perhaps I can make use of your services as well, Mr. Fields. Can you track down a servant girl?"

"I do not mean to appear immodest, but I have only ever failed twice in my endeavors, and those were many years ago. Success will, naturally, depend upon the parameters I am given. Is this an urgent matter?"

"Of some timeliness."

"The other determinant of success is the quality of knowledge I am provided."

"Ah, yes, well the quality in this instance is poor. I do not even know her name."

Mr. Fields was taken aback. "You are unacquainted with the woman you seek?"

"I only know she was a maid of the late wife of Sir Reginald Arthur of Fairgate. Are you familiar with Sir Arthur?"

"No, but if you are, sir, could you not request the name

of the maid from him?"

"From what I understand, Sir Arthur and the maid did not part on good terms."

"I see."

"And I would prefer to keep my inquiry private."

"Of course."

"I know not what documents were kept by the justice of the peace regarding the death of the late Lady Arthur, but you may begin your search there."

"Very good, sir."

"Have you an agreement you wish me to sign before you commence your work for me?"

"No written agreement. Only the word of a gentleman and a deposit of twenty pounds are needed."

"The word of a gentleman being insufficient?"

Mr. Fields cleared his throat. "Well, I have been burned by men I thought were gentlemen."

"Worry not. I will have the funds for you tomorrow."

"Am I permitted, then, to return?"

"Yes, Mr. Washington, you are."

"Thank you, sir."

Charles watched as the man bowed and took his leave. Alone, Charles took in a deep breath. Sir Arthur would not appreciate Charles investigating his past, but Charles had the eerie feeling that he could not pass upon the opportunity.

Chapter Twenty-One

Charles ran a hand through his hair as he stood at the threshold of Madame's chambers. *His* chambers for the sennight. Behind the door, Miss Terrell awaited him.

He was about to put his hand on the door when it opened. Wang stood before him. Charles had long ceased to wonder how Wang always knew of his approach. The man had the eyesight of a hawk and the hearing of a bat.

"Fresh tea waiting for you," Wang said. "Four treasure tea to improve stamina."

Stamina. He supposed he would need it with Miss Terrell. His blood coursed more strongly at the thought.

"*Xie xie*," Charles said, looking beyond his valet into the room.

Upon his entry, Miss Terrell had assumed a proper submissive position. She knelt with her hands clasped behind her and her head bowed. He walked over to the cage, excitement percolating as he observed her lovely naked form. The breasts standing at proud attention. The swell of her hips. The supple thighs. The patch of ebony curls at her groin.

"Good evening, Master," she said.

"Have you been good, Miss Terrell?" he asked as he unbuttoned his coat, for he could feel the heat rising up his neck already.

"I have, Master."

He turned to Wang. "Has she?"

Wang gave a curt nod.

"I am pleased to hear it," Charles said.

Wang assisted him from his coat and waistcoat and into a silk banyan. Charles sat at a writing table. He had letters to pen that he had hoped to complete today, but his meetings with several civic leaders of Porter's Hill had lasted far longer than expected. Of course he had little interest in letters when Miss Terrell knelt a few feet from him, stripped to the buff and looking no less beautiful than a peacock in a gilded cage. Tonight she was his. All his. She was his to command, to discipline, yet the triumph was hers.

He took out paper and dipped pen into ink. The Baron Amherst had taken an interest in China and wished Charles to advise him. Charles suspected Amherst contemplated a second mission to China with the hopes that it would prove more successful than the one led by Macartney, of which Charles' father had been a part.

Wang moved the tea tray to the writing table, bowed and departed. Charles sipped the tea, the same kind that Wang had served to Miss Terrell, as he began composing his letter. It was no easy task, for his cock was distracted, but if he tended to Miss Terrell first, he knew not when he would finish the letter. He could hear her breaths between the sounds of the pen scratching upon paper.

"Permission to sit, Master," she said after several minutes had passed.

"Granted," he replied.

Several more minutes passed.

"Permission to touch myself, Master."

The point of his pen slipped. He wiped at the smear of

ink before responding, "Permission denied."

"Permission to speak."

"Denied," he said, attempting to concentrate upon his letter.

"Permission to move about."

"Very well."

He finished the sentence he was writing, but before long, he could hear her breaths had become pants. Looking over, he saw that she was upon her back in the cage, her hands gripping the bars above her head while she rocked her hips from side to side. She moaned low and soft. Delicious tension flared in his groin as she arched her back. Her breasts, firm with youth, did not flatten, slid but a little to the sides, and remained lovely rising hillocks. Her breath quivered as the Ben Wa balls rolled inside of her.

Bloody hell. There was no way he could finish the letter. Not when he wanted to replace the balls with his cock. He imagined the delightful places the little globes touched.

A knock at the door drew his attention. He knew it to be Wang and wondered how Miss Terrell enjoyed, or failed to enjoy, undressing before the man. He had never before tasked Wang with such an unusual responsibility, but Wang balked at nothing.

"A Mr. Patterson requests your audience," Wang said after entering.

"I know no Patterson."

"He wishes to apply for membership."

Charles glanced at Miss Terrell. "Show him in."

Wang bowed and soon thereafter a pretty young man, dressed to the pink, entered. Mr. Patterson doffed his hat and was about to speak, but upon seeing Miss Terrell, faltered.

Realizing he would have to begin the discourse, Charles

said, "I understand you wish to be a member here, Mr. Patterson."

"Er—yes," the young man said. He spared Charles a glance before returning to stare at Miss Terrell.

Charles indicated a chair. "What of the Red Chrysanthemum interests you, Mr. Patterson?"

He waited several beats. "Mr. Patterson. Mr. Patterson!"

Startled to attention, Patterson tore his gaze from Miss Terrell. "Forgive me. I am most interested in the Red Chrysanthemum."

"Why?"

"Because I have certain, er, predilections."

"Such as?"

Mr. Patterson blushed, making him even more comely. He had the innocent eyes of a doe. "I…I enjoy the company of men, sir."

"There are several molly houses in London. Do they not suit your purposes?"

"I seek men who would be willing…who share…" His attention drifted back to Miss Terrell.

Charles followed his gaze. Miss Terrell had covered herself with her arms.

"Come, Miss Terrell, there is no need to feign modesty when you have none," he said.

She gave him a disgruntled pout before letting her arms fall to her sides.

Charles turned back to Mr. Patterson. "Ever been in a cage before?"

"No." Patterson swallowed. "But I think I should like to try."

"Is this your first visit here?"

"Yes."

"How did you hear of the inn?"

"A fellow at one of the molly houses mentioned the place. Said he was once a member."

"Who was this fellow?"

"A Mr. Knox."

Charles knew the man from his early days at the Red Chrysanthemum. "When were you acquainted with Mr. Knox?"

Patterson had returned to staring at Miss Terrell, who had taken to sucking two of her fingers.

"Mr. Patterson!"

"Forgive me. What was the question?"

Despite the young man's preference for male company, there was an obvious tenting at his crotch.

"Mr. Patterson, we are near capacity with our members. If I am to accept any members, they must be unwavering in their dedication and earnestness."

Charles pulled out a sheaf of papers from a drawer, stood, and handed them to Mr. Patterson. "These statements describe the conditions and requisites with which all members must adhere. Take the time to study them. If, after reflection, you are still committed to becoming a member, you may seek a formal application for membership."

"Thank you, sir."

Patterson received the papers and, realizing the meeting was at an end, stood and replaced his hat.

"Good evening to you, Mr. Patterson."

"Good—good evening, sir."

Wang opened the door for Mr. Patterson.

"You may retire for the night, Wang," Charles informed his valet. "Thank you for your assistance."

With a nod, Wang followed Mr. Patterson and closed

the door behind him. Charles turned to Miss Terrell and folded his arms.

"Did I give you leave to suckle your fingers, Miss Terrell?"

Chapter Twenty-Two

Terrell resisted the desire to squirm beneath Master Gallant's unflinching stare. She should have known better, but she felt like a child desperate for attention. Gallant had kept her caged, unable to touch herself or relieve the tension pulsating in her body, while he wrote his bloody letters and conducted a bloody meeting. While she sat naked in a cage for anyone to ogle!

"Forgive me, Master," she said, dutifully lowering her gaze. "My body craves for an orifice to be filled, preferably with an object long and hard."

She sensed his eyes widening.

"May I make amends by sucking your cock?"

He deliberated before saying, "I will reward you with cock, for you did well following Wang's instructions."

"If I may, it was quite demeaning, Master, making me strip to the buff before your Oriental, pleasuring myself before him, and allowing him to insert these wicked balls inside my cunnie."

"It was not my intention to demean. Wang may be my valet, but I hold him in great esteem. I should have found my death in China were it not for him."

"I was unaware of this. But if it pleases you, I will do anything you wish with Mr. Wang. If you wish to reward him for his service to you, I will take his cock into my mouth—or perhaps you would wish to watch him fuck me in the arse?"

Stifling a groan, he untied the sash of his robe and approached the cage. She came to her knees in quick anticipation. He presented her his fall. Reaching through the bars, she undid all his buttons to reveal his glorious member. She licked her lips at its stiff length. How she had hungered for his cock all day! She admired its slight curve, the ridges, and beautiful flared head.

"May I touch it?" she asked.

"You may."

She grasped his erection and shivered. Her other hand cupped his cods. He grunted. She slid her hand down the shaft and, pressing her face to the bars, licked him from his scrotum to the sensitive underside of the crown. He took in a swift breath. Slowly, she drew him into her mouth.

His thickness, pulsing inside of her, tasted delectable. She sucked his cock ravenously, as if taking him could relieve her own yearning. Though her body craved to have his cock in a different orifice, she was content at present to wrap her lips about his shaft. His arousal felt divine, and she took no small satisfaction in knowing she could command such an effect from him.

She took him into her throat, her saliva gliding his way. His grunts, her own heavy breathing through her nose, her cheeks pressed against the bars, the risk of choking as his cock penetrated harder and faster, the balls moving inside of her, all enflamed the heat between her legs.

She began pulling away, for she wanted to ask his permission to touch herself, to address the ache in her suffering cunnie, but he reached through the cage and fisted his hand into her hair, holding her in place while he thrust deeper into her. She convulsed a little when the tip of his cock struck the top of her throat, but she righted herself just as his paroxysm loomed. He bucked his hips faster, his hand clenching tighter in her hair. With a roar, he spent inside her mouth. She swallowed his thick emission, for she could do nothing else, but she relished the taste of him, found victory in the unleashing of his seed. She continued to suckle him till his cock could take no more.

Releasing her, he leaned an arm upon the top of his cage. He shuddered.

"*My God*," he breathed. "That is a fair wondrous mouth you have, Miss Terrell."

She licked her lips. "Thank you for your cock, Master."

"You are most welcome, Miss Terrell."

He righted himself and buttoned his trousers. She waited expectantly, wondering what he would do next. She hoped he would kiss her or free her from the cage.

He did neither.

Instead, he went back to the writing table and, sitting down, took up his pen. She smiled wryly to herself. Now she understood the nature of her discipline.

Undaunted, she asked, "How else might I pleasure you, Master?"

He did not look up. "You may be quiet and still while I finish this letter."

She groaned in aggravation, then silently cursed him. Desire screamed in her veins. Having his cock had soothed the edges of her arousal, for she had an object to focus her verve upon, but now that she was returned to empty-handedness, her frustration was worse than before. Those damned balls had caressed her cunnie to distraction. She needed to touch herself.

Perhaps he would be done soon.

She sat in her cage and watched as he wrote. For a

while, she was content to admire him. He had a distinguished profile, and she liked the wave of his golden locks. She liked the shape of his mouth and how ardently it kissed. She would like nothing more than to have those lips over every inch of her body. The pressure swelled in her loins.

She decided to lie down and close her eyes, that she might turn her thoughts away from titillation. She could always dwell upon the her time in Barbados, but try as she might, her mind would not ignore the agitation swirling in her body, her wetness between her legs. Her cunnie pulsed and clenched. And a new sensation had reared its head.

She needed to piss.

She returned to a sitting position. Was he not yet done with his bloody letter?

She shifted restlessly for several more minutes, during which he remained focused upon his letter, not once glancing her way. She should not have had that second cup of tea.

"Master, may I be let out of the cage?" she asked. "I've a need to use Madame's commode."

When he did not respond, she added, "Or a chamber pot would do."

"I am not yet done with my letter," he answered.

She drew in a sharp breath. Did he truly mean to deny her? Surely he meant only to tease her a little.

But the minutes dragged on. She squeezed her legs together, not knowing which urgency now needed addressing more.

"Master, I am in some hurry," she tried.

To her relief, he set down his pen. "Are you?"

She nodded emphatically.

He approached the cage and lifted the top. She was

never happier to be able to stand. He assisted her out of the cage, but instead of fetching a chamber pot, he went to the writing table and picked up a pair of thin sticks from his tea tray. She stood waiting by the cage, perplexed.

"In China," he said as he wrapped string about the sticks, "these are used as eating utensils."

A strange manner of eating, she thought to herself. What these sticks had to do with her need to piss, she could not guess. He had tied the sticks together in two places. He approached her and took one of her nipples between his thumb and forefinger. She moaned as he tugged it to hardness. A thrill went through her, shooting from her nipple to somewhere deep in her cunnie. She grasped the balls, glad to have something inside of her.

He pinched and rolled her nipple, making her moan long and low with need. He then pried open the center of the sticks and snapped them over her hardened bud.

She cried out as the sticks pinched her sensitive nipple.

He took her second nipple into his mouth. She arched herself into the warm wetness enclosing her. The sweet torture upon one bud contrasted with the sharp pressure upon the other made her mind spin and reel. He went back to the writing table and picked up another pair of sticks, which he tied together. This time she knew what was coming and braced herself for the pinching upon her nipple. She breathed into the pain, welcoming it as pleasure. She had nearly forgotten the urgency of her bladder.

Taking her by the hand, he led her to the bed. The balls jostled inside her with every step.

"Kneel up here."

He indicated a spot near the edge of the bed. That did not bode well. Was he not going to let her relieve herself?

He gestured toward the wall facing the bed and she saw herself in a large mirror. Lust flared at the site of her own body, naked, her nipples trapped in the odd dining implements, her cheeks flushed from arousal. Gallant knelt behind her upon the bed. He had removed the sash from his robe and used it to tie her wrists behind her back.

"Keep your gaze upon the looking glass," he instructed.

Cupping her breasts, he rolled the orbs. She sighed in pleasure even while the sticks pinched her nipples and discomfort persisted in her bladder. He dropped a hand languidly down her torso to her mound. She gasped when his fingers slid past her clitoris.

"Please, no," she whispered when he touched her piss-hole, aggravating that need there.

Ignoring her, he continued to rub between your legs. She could not decide if the sensations he stoked with his digits were delightful or aggravating or both.

Both. She wanted to clench her thighs together.

"Please, Master, may I be allowed to relieve myself?"

"Not yet."

Her breath crumbled. He rubbed harder, faster. Her legs begin to quake, which caused the balls to move. She strained to be still. She exhaled an agonized cry when he inserted two of his fingers into her quim and agitated them quickly, making the balls dance.

It was too much. The pain in her nipples had dissipated but it was nothing compared to the pressure in her groin, exacerbated by his fingers and the balls.

"Whatever you do, Miss Terrell, do not piss upon Madame's bed."

"Then stop frigging me," she pleaded.

He clasped her body to his with one arm while his other hand, buried between your legs, continued its maddening torture.

She wanted both to spend and to piss. As she did not know that she could refrain from soiling the bed, she begged, "Please stop."

"What is your safety word?"

Safety word?!

"I don't remember!"

She could no longer think. No matter how she bucked her hips, and doing so only worsened the movement of the balls, she could not escape his ministration. The pressure between her legs intensified. God help her…

"Do not dare piss upon the bed," he said.

She could only wail helplessly in response. Her body knew not what to do against the assault. The tightness inside her body threatened to explode.

And then it did.

Liquid streamed from her as shudders racked her body. She no longer knew if it might be piss. Her body had been granted the ecstasy it had craved for several long hours. She jerked against him as spasms ricocheted throughout her, blasting her with astounding intensity.

When, at last, she emerged from the depths of her paroxysm, she collapsed against him, gulping for air as if she had been submerged in water. In the darkness of her closed eyes, she could hear her heartbeat and felt his chest behind her expand. For the moment, if she were never allowed to spend again, her body would have accepted such a sentence without remorse.

She sighed and thought she felt the tender kiss of his lips upon her temple.

Chapter Twenty-Three

His cock could not be harder. He remained as he was, with her body slumped against him, allowing her time to recover. Nothing could be more arousing, yet more satisfying than the sight of her body destroyed by rapture. He derived immense pleasure in seeing her spend much as a man might, with a stream of liquid. He could tell from its scent that it was not urine and found it curious that a woman could ejaculate as well. Much of the emission had sprayed on the rug below, and he reminded himself that he ought to inform Wang of it.

His cock throbbed as he looked upon her beautiful body with perfectly full and rounded breasts, the loveliest navel, the flared hips...the combination of these elements exceeding the sum of the parts. He admired the chopsticks trapping her nipples one last time before removing the implements.

She sighed in relief before her eyes opened in alarm, and she bolted upright.

"I need to piss," she declared. She looked at him in desperation.

He swept her off the bed and carried her to the closet that housed the commode. He set her down upon her feet. She did not wait for him to leave before she sat down to attend the call of nature. He watched, desire continuing to churn in his groin. Was there anything she did he would not find arousing? He imagined watching her do the laundry. That she was naked while pushing garments down a washing board into a bucket of water made the scene quite arousing.

"Thank you, Master," she said when done, her countenance awash in relief.

She still had her arms pinioned. Walking over, he removed the sash and returned it to his banyan.

"I think a bath would be in order, Miss Terrell," he said.

Her eyes widened at the prospect of using Madame's large cast-iron tub. "Yes, Master."

He gave her his banyan though he believed he would never tire of seeing her naked body.

Back in the bedchamber, he took a deep breath. He had wanted to turn her around as soon as she stood, bend her over the commode, and fuck her. But he thought a little respite in order for her. After ringing for Wang, he sat once more at the writing table. He had yet to finish his letter to Lord Amherst.

"Have some more tea, Miss Terrell," he said.

She sidled over, her face still glowing from her paroxysm.

"I wonder if your tea is more potent than gin?" she murmured as she poured herself a cup.

He grinned. "For certain, it is far more healthful."

"Is that how you are able to sustain the hardness of your cock so impressively?"

"It has improved since I first came across it in a brothel in Canton."

Walking around, she took her place before him, leaning against the writing table. "Canton?"

He watched how her thick, pouting lips wrapped the cup she held. "China."

Wang appeared then, and Charles bid him draw a bath.

"What are the women of China like?" Miss Terrell asked when Wang had left to fetch hot water.

"You mean their appearance?"

"If you wish."

"It varies. China is vast. In the north, the women are more pale of skin. In the south, they are smaller. But they all possess the same straight black hair and dark eyes."

"And their nature?"

"In the brothels, they are deferential. Docile. They would make good submissives. Unlike willful blackamoors."

"I think you would find me far less pleasurable were I docile."

He considered her statement and found he would have to agree. She certainly would not have succeeded in seducing him if she had been more demure. His cock twitched.

She set her tea down and slid to her knees. "Confess, you enjoy my wantonness. Master."

His pulse quickened as she settled herself between his legs.

"My boldness," she said, resting her arms over his legs. Her fingers walked their way toward his fall. "My unabashed fondness for cock."

Heat swirled in his groin. His breath became uneven. Damnation. He needed an antidote to Miss Terrell.

Just then Wang entered, carrying two large kettles with steam rising from their spouts. Remaining where she was, Terrell smiled impishly at Charles. He fisted his hand in her hair. Hers had not the softness of Miss Greta or Miss Lily, but he could grip the thick curls well.

"Behave yourself," he said.

She lowered her lashes. "Yes, Master."

He slid his hand to the side of her face and brushed a thumb along her lower lip before pressing the digit into her mouth. She closed her lips about his thumb and sucked. His pulse skipped. He moved his thumb, simulating the motions his cock would have wished, before swirling it atop her tongue and feeling the inside of a cheek.

"May I, Master?" she asked when Wang had departed with the emptied kettles.

"You would suck my cock again?" he returned.

"Indeed. I think I shall never tire of your cock, Master Gallant."

His cock reared its head at her words. It was more than willing to sink into her mouth once more.

"Is it possible you will never tire?" he murmured.

"I once sucked ten cocks in succession."

He frowned. It was not what he wanted to hear, but he could not resist asking, "Ten in succession?"

"Mr. Tremayne had his friends from the neighboring plantations visiting one evening."

That bloody overseer. Charles still felt the desire to kick the shit from the man.

"What manner of atrocity did he threaten you with?"

"He need not have threatened. I willingly attended all the overseers and their friends."

He stared at her in disbelief.

"You think me a horrible hedge whore," she said, "and so I am. I trade my favors for a better situation in life. How many men would not do the same, were they in my place?"

"I cannot answer for all, but for myself, it would be no easy matter to take ten cocks into my mouth lest I desired to."

"Indeed. Mr. Tremayne would have forced me to pleasure his friends—and whupped me if I dared refuse. I learned early 'tis far better to acquiesce than to fight the inevitable. I have seen other slaves sobbing as they took cock. I would not be rendered into such misery. I took cock willingly and was rewarded for my desire to please."

Charles said nothing. She spoke with reason. More than that, she had taken a hideous situation and refused to be conquered by it. *I would not be rendered into such misery.* She had made an activity that most would loath to suffer into one of opportunity. In the face of subjugation, she had maintained herself in possession of a sort of will, as if she had had the freedom of choice.

There was no mitigating that which had been imposed upon her was ungodly. Her reaction to the atrocities that befell her stemmed from delusion or, perhaps, an exceptional ability to conform her mind to what was needed. Oddly, it reminded Charles of the monks in the mountains of China, who practiced putting their minds above matter. The set of her mind enabled her to persevere where others might have perished.

"But you have not always acquiesced," he said quietly.

"When I took cock, no one suffered for what I did, but my sister—half-sister—had a more delicate constitution. She was much younger, and I could not so easily hand her to Mr. Tremayne."

Charles shook his head at the valor of a woman he would have, moments ago, dubbed a flagrant whore. Slavery had made whoring her only means of improving her situation. What institution could be more dreadful? What institution could make whoring the better option? Remembering the stipulations of Mathilda Brentwood, he shifted uneasily in his chair.

"I did not mean to vex you," Miss Terrell said. She reached for his fall. "But I can make amends."

He lifted her and set her on his thigh. "Is your sister still in Barbados?"

She seemed to stare into the past. "She is at peace."

Charles closed his eyes. He drew her closer. "I'm sorry."

"While I was the property of the one who gambled, I had heard she had been married to Cain, a fellow slave. I thought this was good, as Cain was a team driver and slept in better quarters than most of the other slaves."

"But I take it even a husband could not protect her from Mr. Tremayne."

"Mr. Tremayne had to sanction their union. Before Mr. Terrell was to depart from England, I sought to send her word. That was when I learned she had come to her death by accident in the boiling house."

"Have you any family remaining in Barbados?"

"My mother died when I was young. I knew not my father. Some said it might have been the master himself."

Charles paled. "The plantation owner whom you had congress with?"

She shrugged. "Or perhaps it was Mr. Tremayne. My mother never told me."

She spoke with dispassion, but he felt sick. He tightened his hold on her. "Thank God you are removed from that hell." Turning to a lighter subject, he said, "By the quality of your speech, one would not suspect you to have been formerly a slave."

Her countenance lightened, and she was clearly proud of this accomplishment. "Mr. Terrell took the time to improve my speech when he could. My skills in the sugar fields were of no use here. I worked as a scullery maid for a short period, but I could live far better if I employed the *other* skills I had acquired. When I became more presentable, I could attach myself as a courtesan. I thought it possible to become as well-situated as any woman of the *ton* if I wore the same clothes and talked in the same manner. Now that I have my freedom, why should I allow my blackness to condemn me to poverty and wretchedness?"

He looked at her with no small amount of awe. "If you applied yourself to learning to read as well as you have applied yourself to improving discourse, it would not take you long at all to master reading."

Her eyes shone brightly. "Do you speak in earnest?"

"I think you capable of anything you set your mind to." He saw the flicker of a new emotion in her face. He cupped her chin. "Let it be known you are a remarkable woman, Miss Terrell, in many, many ways."

He caressed her bottom lip once more, then, inclining his head, captured it in his mouth. She allowed him to claim her with a long, smoldering kiss before returning with her own verve.

She grasped his head in both her hands with, it seemed, more passion, and his body responded, warming to the way her tongue flitted between his lips. Though he intended she should be the submissive, he liked that she could be an equal partner in the dance between their mouths. She did not merely receive his kiss but returned it with a heady forcefulness that aroused more than it unnerved.

Cupping the back of her head, he pressed his tongue farther into her, wanting to taste the depths of her mouth. Their first kiss, he had sought the taste of Miss Greta upon her, but now, he favored the intoxication of Miss Terrell. Wanton, bold, ravenous, relentless, profound.

When he chanced to look past her, he saw Wang standing before the writing table. He tried to speak, but Miss Terrell still clung to his mouth, softly biting his lower lip.

"Terrell," he mumbled, but she covered his mouth, licking and sucking as if she had not eaten in days. 'Terrell!"

She did not stop so he found and pinched her nipple. With a yelp, she released his mouth, then realized that he looked past her.

"The bath is ready," Wang informed them.

"Thank you."

"Do you—"

"No, thank you," Charles replied quickly.

Wang bowed and took his leave. If the two of them had not visited the brothels of Canton together, Charles might have felt some embarrassment at the witness of his valet, but he hid nothing from Wang. He wasn't sure he could even if he tried.

Scooping up Miss Terrell, he carried her to the closet where the bath awaited. He set her down, and they resumed kissing. He knew not where his newfound hunger for her arose. At first, his arousal seemed to stem from the natural urges of his sex when presented with a lovely form. He had been curious, his vanity stoked by her determined seduction. Then there was the need to exert his manhood, to reclaim his dominion. But at present, his desire comprised more than these elements. Yes, he wanted to possess her. But worship, too. With his lips, his hands, his cock.

He slid the banyan from her and, cupping a buttock, fit

her naked body to his, pressing his erection to her. She ground herself against it as her hands loosened his cravat. He pulled back.

"Will you not bathe, too, Master?" she asked.

He had not intended to, had never bathed with a woman before, but it would be fruitless to resist. Especially with Miss Terrell. With her aid, he divested his clothing one by one. She caressed the parts of him laid bare, running her hands up his legs to his hips as he stood in nothing but his shirt. His blood pulsed quickly, and his cock bobbed for her attention, but he urged her into the bath before the water turned tepid.

"Yes, Master," she said and stepped into the tub.

He glimpsed the scars upon her back before she turned to look at him. He was glad she no longer felt the need to hide her disfigurement from him, though he could not forebear thinking it a shame that such a lovely back should come to such ruin.

Tossing his shirt aside, he joined her. He sat down and pulled her before him. His cock slid along her arse, and he wondered how soon he might claim her final orifice. He reached for soap, lathered his hands, and drew them along her arms. He spread the soap over her chest, her breasts. She gasped when he grazed her nipples. He caressed her belly, the length of her legs, before returning a hand between her thighs. She leaned her back against his chest, sliding deeper into the water as he fondled her.

"Did you and your Oriental—" she began.

"Wang."

"Wang. Did you and he share women?"

"Why do you ask?"

"I know few valets who would have been rendered the tasks you required of him tonight."

"Hmmm. I imagine any number of valets would have been happy to assume his duties tonight." He played with her clitoris as he spoke. "Wang is no ordinary valet to me. Though he seems content in my employment, he deserves more."

"If he desired, would you permit him to fuck me?"

Charles stiffened.

"I could accommodate the both of you."

"Do you wish to?"

"If it pleases you, Master Gallant."

She faced away from him, and he could not see her countenance. He would have liked to grant Wang anything the man desired, but Charles preferred not to share Miss Terrell at the moment.

"I wish to do anything you please," she added.

"Anything."

"*Anything* and *everything.*"

His cock throbbed. "Are you certain?"

She turned to face him, her wet body sliding along his. "Yes. Do with me what you will. I want to know the extent of your wickedness, Master Gallant."

His voice became hoarse. "Do you recall your safety word, Miss Terrell?"

She thought for a moment. "Fanny."

"Good." He put his hand to the back of her head. "Take a deep breath, then take my cock into your mouth."

She hesitated for a second but then smiled. "Gladly, Master Gallant."

After seeing her take in a breath, he guided her into the water. She cupped his sack as she fitted her mouth over his shaft. As always, it felt *divine.* The texture of her tongue pressed upon him—now rubbing along his length—was finer than the softest velvet.

When he thought she needed air, he brought her back up. Water dripped from her face, and the sparkle in her eyes made him want to melt in the bath. After she took another large breath, he gently pushed her back into the water. This time she sucked at his cock.

My God.

He moved her head up and down his erection. Bubbles of air popped along the surface of the water. When there was no more, he lifted her head above the water. She came up gasping for air, her luscious lips parted.

"Once more," he said, pushing her under.

She closed her mouth tight about him. He lifted his hips and pressed more of him into her. She grunted in the water but took as much of him as she could, given the confines of the tub. She sucked at him but, without air, could only sustain the motion for so long, though with his hand still at her head, he kept her in place. Desperation for air growing, she gripped his cock harder with one hand while the other gripped his arm. He let her up when he saw her knuckles turn white.

She emerged gasping and gulping in air. Not waiting for her to recover, he flipped her over and guided his cock into her cunnie. Her head fell against his chest. Her rump pressed against his pelvis. Her hot, wet cunnie clenched upon his cock. Wrapping an arm over her bosom, he pumped himself in and out of her. Her moans were short between heavy breaths.

Reaching his free hand between her legs, he stroked her.

Her ascent swift, she grasped the sides of the tub. "M-M…"

He palmed a breast.

"M-May…" she tried.

"You may spend, Miss Terrell."

With a cry, she erupted into spasms, her limbs thrashing the water out of the tub. He had to hold her down to keep her from bucking off his cock, for his own release was imminent. The flexing of her cunnie against his cock threw him over the edge. That delicious pressure collecting in his loins shot through his cock, unleashing its seed into her.

"I see that breath play agrees with you, Miss Terrell," he murmured.

"*You* agree with me, Master Gallant," she replied with a sigh.

As he relished the sensations of her body slumped upon his, his cock softening inside her pulsing cunnie, the water, no longer hot but warm, wrapping them both, he answered her silently.

And you with me.

Chapter Twenty-Four

Her legs straddled over him, Terrell rolled her hips, grateful that his cock could harden once more, though he had spent but moments ago in the bath.

Atop him upon the bed, she possessed the control she had been denied earlier, though she had enjoyed the lack of control, even the lack of breath as he had dunked her head into the water. The excitement, the desperation arising from the deprivation of air, was more scintillating than she would have guessed. Her last experience with breath play had been rather terrifying, but she trusted Gallant, even more than she had trusted Mr. Terrell. She wanted Master Gallant to test her limits, to put her body through the most exquisite of tortures. The sweet sparkle of desire in his eyes was reward enough.

He gripped her thighs, aiding her motion. She caressed herself and presented him a view of her breasts bounding up and down. He grasped one, making her moan as he rubbed his thumb over the nipple. She put her hands upon his chest to give herself greater leverage. He groaned as she rode him with increased vigor, thrusting his hips to meet her descent. She savored the depths to which his cock penetrated. No one filled her as well as him, though she had taken cocks longer and thicker. But his was, by far, the best.

Pleasure waved through her loins, pulling her higher and higher to that summit, one which she had already attained numerous times but which she now craved as if she had never spent once. But she tried to pace herself. Because he had not voiced permission for her to spend. And because she wanted to make him spend first. She wanted to make him desperate to spend, as he had done to her. She worked the muscles of her cunnie on his shaft and received his groan with satisfaction.

For a man fair of hair and complexion, he was the most handsome man she had ever known. From the thickness of his lashes to the shape of his mouth, there was nothing she did not admire. Most of all, she adored the smolder of arousal upon his physiognomy. The veins in his neck tightened as he grasped her by the hips and shoved himself deeper and harder. She gasped, feeling like a rag doll, for she could do nothing while he held her and battered his cock into her.

"Yes! Spend, Master!" she cried.

He slowed his thrusting. Their gazes locked, and she knew that *he* knew what she attempted. He grinned.

"We shall see, shall we?" he replied.

Without notice, he flipped her off him and onto her knees. Kneeling behind her, he sank his cock back in. She moaned. In this position, she could offer little resistance. The angle of his cock touched her most sensitive place, making her tremble. He slapped a buttock. Her cunnie clenched upon him in response. Slowly, he began to draw his length in and out of her. She dug her fingers into the bedclothes below. With other men, she tried to spend as quickly as possible, not knowing if they would attend to her after they had spent. She had never before tried *not* to spend.

"Fuck my arse," she mumbled.

He smacked her arse instead. She groaned in delight.

Perhaps she should relent. But she wanted a little of the power she had had when she had seduced him into succumbing. She shoved her backside at his pelvis. He responded by reaching a hand around her hip to fondle her clitoris.

Noooo.

Her legs grew weak. The stimulation was too much. She buried her face into the linen and tried to caress his cock with her cunnie. He felt it and responded by pounding his cock into her. She could not control her screams as she found herself pommeled into the bed. God help her. The pleasure threatened to shatter her body into thousands of pieces.

Just as she lost the last of her resistance, his cock surged inside of her. His pelvis slammed against her arse, his cods swung at her folds. He shuddered and jerked against her as her body surrendered to the immense euphoria. She felt the reverberation to the tips of her toes. Her body felt unable to contain its force as it sought freedom in her screams, her clenching, her quaking.

She collapsed into the bed, and he atop her. Her cunnie throbbed. Pulses went up and down the insides of her legs, and it was some time before she felt she had regained full possession of her limbs.

"My God," he breathed after he had rolled off of her.

He pulled her into the crook of his arm. She lay her head upon his chest, comparing the heavy beating of his heart to hers. His body was quite warm from the exertions, his skin damp from perspiration. But he felt wonderful. She had never known lying with a man could offer such contentment. She had seen a different look in his eyes tonight. He had looked at her differently. In admiration, almost. To have the esteem of Charles Gallant was of no small significance.

She sighed with the gratification of a heart filled.

Chapter Twenty-Five

Terrell woke to the luxury of silk bedclothes, her head upon a soft down pillow. A woman of thrift for the most part, the proprietress spared little expense for her own bedchamber. Terrell rubbed her legs along the linen and felt the weight of a blanket upon her. She had spent the night with Master Gallant. In Madame's bed. Or, for the time being, *his* bed.

In the middle of the night, she had thought to return to her own quarters. They had both drifted to sleep, but he had not specified that she could share his bed. She had not set one foot out of bed, however, when she felt a hand grasping her hair, pulling her back.

"I did not grant you permission to leave the bed."

Her pulse had quickened at the surprise. As he held her hair tight, she could not turn her head to see him. But she felt him. Her bare arse rested against his thigh.

"What if I needed to piss? Would you require I should request your blessing?"

"You require my permission, Miss Terrell. At all times when in my presence. When I am absent, you will behave yourself."

"In what manner?"

"Ask yourself if I would approve. Let that be your guide."

"What if I suppose incorrectly?"

"Then you will be punished when I return."

She drew in a sharp breath. "You are exacting, Master Gallant."

"Then suppose correctly."

For a brief moment, she had wondered if she had erred in seeking to be his submissive, but it pleased her that he cared enough to demand her behavior in his absence.

Then all reserve had been wiped away when he had pulled her to him. Her derriere had brushed against the hardness of his cock. In the darkness, he had fitted himself between her thighs and taken her while she lay wrapped in his arms. He had cupped a breast but engaged in none of the ceremony that usually preceded his penetration. But none was needed. Upon feeling his arousal, her body had been instantly receptive. The angle had not been an easy one, but the sensations unfurling from between her legs had been exquisite. And when he had put a hand to her mons to stroke her as he ground his hips into her arse, she had doubted her forbearance. To her relief, he had not waited long before granting her permission to spend.

She did not think she had spent a more marvelous night.

She blinked away the last of her slumber and realized Gallant, completely dressed, sat at the tea table, observing her. The curtains were drawn, but the light slipping through was white, indicating the morning was fairly advanced. He must have dressed in the anteroom, for she had heard nothing.

"Good morning," he greeted. It seemed he had been in deep thought, but if he entertained any regret for accepting her submission, he displayed none of it.

"Good morning," she returned, relieved when he returned her smile. She sat up in bed. "Have you been awake long?"

"An hour or so." Rising from his seat, he retrieved his banyan for her. "I will ring for breakfast."

"Thank you."

She slid into the robe while he rang for Wang. Covered, she went to sit before the table while he drew aside the curtains. He then poured her a cup of coffee.

"Pray, let me not keep you from your day," she said.

"I had sent word yesterday with my apologies that I would be unable to keep my early morning engagement." He sat down opposite her. "I had anticipated a late night."

Her heart fluttered, and she flushed. She took a sip of coffee. "Did you?"

"I did. Though the level of activity far surpassed my expectations."

His charming grin made her sigh. She drew her legs onto the armchair and took another sip.

His gaze took in all of her. "You will wear me down to nothing before the sennight is over."

She could not resist smiling at the compliment. "And you I, Master Gallant."

"Your sex has the advantage, Miss Terrell."

"Yes, but you are welcome to attempt its demise."

His brows rose. Her pulse quickened. If he were not dressed so finely, his cravat perfectly tied, she might have launched herself at him.

He poured coffee for himself. "The undertaking might well be worth the prospect of my defeat."

A knock at the door announced the arrival of Wang with breakfast. Rather than the toast or porridge she consumed most days, she was treated to ham, eggs and beans. Hungry, she fell upon the food in earnest.

He watched her eat for a moment before saying, "I hope you are fed properly here at the inn."

She nodded as she swallowed a mouthful of toast with beans. "I do not starve here, but I am accustomed to eating as much as I can when afforded the opportunity."

At his quizzical expression, she added, "Till I started working in the Great House and was provided meals, food was not always easy to come by."

He was taken aback. "Did they not feed you on the plantation?"

"We were given rations of breadfruit."

"An economical sustenance," he said wryly.

"And salted cod from time to time, but most often it was rancid. At night, we would steal from the neighboring plantations or sometimes from the skilled slaves, for they received double rations. I remember my mother coming by yam once. It was delicious! I remember I wanted to save some for her, but she bid me eat it all, and I was so very hungry."

"Were you allowed a day of rest?"

"Sundays. Lest it was crop time, when we worked as long as there was light sufficient to see. July and August were hardest."

"I take it the heat was insufferable in those months?"

"It was not the heat I dreaded the most but the snakes and rats. In July and August, we prepared the land for planting. The uncut cane hid untold numbers of the vermin. I've been bitten more times than I can count. Once, Mr. Tremayne estimated over three thousand rats had been caught in that year alone." She shivered in disgust. "But being bitten by a rat is not as treacherous as being gouged by the machetes used to cut the grass and shrubs."

"Were you harmed?"

"No, but others have been."

"Did it happen often?"

"Every year."

He was silent, allowing her to eat. After a few minutes, he asked, "When did you begin working in the fields?"

"About nine years of age, I think. Before then, I was part of the Hogmeat Gang."

"Hogmeat Gang?"

"Comprised of the old, the weak and children. We weeded the gardens and scavenged for food for the animals."

"When does a child start working?"

"Four years of age."

He appeared troubled, for he rose and began a slow pacing behind his chair. She slowed her chewing. She had never talked of her life in Barbados to anyone before, yet conversation came easily with Master Gallant. And she found his interest gratifying.

He retook his seat and rubbed his temples, silence settling between them before she set down her napkin and said, "I hope I've not vexed you. I'm sorry."

"No, no," he replied. "I should not have asked you to recount the misery of your life as a slave. It is only...I wished to understand the circumstances of slavery."

"They are not circumstances I would wish upon anyone," she said with quiet resolve.

He looked away, a sigh of discontent escaping his nostrils. He murmured, "We ought have abolished more than the trading of slaves."

"Surely that day will come. If you are elected to Parliament, could you not support slavery's abolition?"

He shifted uncomfortably. She stared at him. Though they had touched upon the subject before, she asked a more direct question this time. "You would support abolition, would you not?"

"It is not so simple."

She furrowed her brow. There must be more to Parliament than she understood. "Why not?"

"First, I am not yet a Member of Parliament."

"But when you are elected—"

"*If* I am elected, and there is no guarantee lest…"

She could see he was deeply troubled, but she pressed, "Lest?"

"I require the support of at least one party."

"Sir Arthur."

"He is one option."

"Does he not support the abolition of slavery?"

"He has no strong opinion on the matter. His interests lie elsewhere, and while we share these interests in common, his approach differs from mine. He is unlikely to support me if I refuse to follow his lead."

"And you cannot win without him."

"It would be quite difficult, but there is some hope if I can secure the endorsement of the Brentwood family, but they want nothing of abolition at present and have made it a condition of their support."

Terrell stared into her lap, trying to make sense of his situation. It was plain he was conflicted.

"You must choose between Sir Arthur and the Brentwoods."

"I cannot be another man's puppet. I should have no desire to serve in Parliament if that were the case. The Brentwoods agree that abolition is an eventuality. They ask only for time."

"Time? What length of time?"

"Ten, fifteen years. If I were successfully elected, I could support amelioration; laws that could improve the life of slaves and make criminal their mistreatment, till such a time arises that complete abolition can be confirmed."

A knock sounded. It was Wang.

"Shall I have your horse saddled?" the man asked.

"Yes," Gallant answered, turning to her as Wang took his leave. "Come. I will assist in your dress."

She raised playful brows. "You wish to play my dressing maid?"

"Admittedly, I am as likely to *dis*robe you, but I do have engagements to attend today."

He smiled, and she was glad to see the anguish depart his countenance. How she wished that she could ease, with permanence, his distress!

"Do these engagements require your timeliness?" she inquired, sauntering over to where he stood. She began lowering herself to her knees. "Or may you be a little tardy?"

He groaned but pulled her up. Undaunted, she put her hand to his crotch.

"You will cease this wayward behavior, Miss Terrell," he hissed.

"I only wish to please my Master and start his morning with a little *gratification*."

She let her fingers brush his length.

His gaze bore into her as he held her. "I will enjoy seeing your arse turn crimson tonight."

Reluctantly, she withdrew her hand. Only then did he release her. Though she would have liked to taste his cock, she was satisfied that there was to be another night with Master Gallant.

Chapter Twenty-Six

And where were you last night?" asked Sarah from her bed, where George played with the wooden toy horse that Terrell had bought and mended for him.

Terrell could have beamed in response as she pretended to be quite engaged in her small wardrobe. Master Gallant had assisted her into her clothing from the night before, avenging himself for her moment of insubordination by caressing her breasts and combing his fingers through the hair at her mons after he had removed the banyan from her. Her body warmed and aggravated, she wanted none of the garments he had proceeded to dress her in.

"I will not require you to speak his name," Sarah relented with a wry smile, "but perhaps you will know if Master Gallant has departed the inn yet this morning?"

"He has," Terrell answered, selecting a fresh shift and turning around. It was difficult to contain the joy that had led her to return to her room with such lightness that her feet felt as if they had grown wings. With Miss Ruth, she would have divulged every detail, but though Miss Sarah was no novice at the Red Chrysanthemum, she was still too much of a lady to Terrell.

"My, my," Sarah sniffed. "I think I've never seen you flush in such fashion. Your countenance fair glows with bliss."

Did it? Terrell paused, for she could not recollect the last time she had felt such…happiness.

"Well, what shall you do now?" Sarah asked as she searched for a handkerchief.

Terrell returned a perplexed expression.

"You've two men vying for your attentions. Will you forsake Sir Arthur then?"

Remembering Sir Arthur cast a shadow upon her newfound sentiments, but she was not ready to decline the opportunity the man presented.

"I know not that Master Gallant has more than a passing interest for me," she deflected.

"Does he not? He seemed quite determined to find you last night. There was a concern there that did not signify a 'passing interest'."

Terrell recalled the way Gallant had looked at her this morning. As no other man had looked at her. But it did not signify if it could not endure.

"When Sir Arthur returns, Master Gallant will renounce me once again. He has no desire to displease Sir Arthur."

"Yes, I had nearly forgotten the election." Sarah heaved a large sigh. "It is unfortunate timing and circumstance that his fate should rest in the hands of Sir Arthur. Parliament deserves and needs a man with his qualities."

Terrell sat down on her own bed. Sir Arthur owned half of Porter's Hill. Having once been a courtesan to a Member of Parliament, she understood how elections worked in such a borough.

"There is no other way for Master Gallant to win?" she wondered.

"I think it unlikely. From what I have read in the

papers, Gallant is expected to have Sir Arthur's support."

But in the little interaction she had had with Sir Arthur, Terrell knew him to be temperamental. Arthur had forbid her to entertain the attentions of another man and would likely consider Gallant as culpable as she.

"When Sir Arthur returns, Gallant will be done with me," she said, rising to choose her finest petticoats and the gown of blue she had worn the night he had read to her in the dining hall. "Till then, we shall enjoy each other's company."

Sarah blew her nose into her handkerchief. "Are you certain he will wish to be done with you?"

"He is a man of sense more than sensibility, is he not? As you have said, it is curious he has not found a proper young woman of the *ton* to marry. Unlike Sir Arthur, Char—Gallant is not yet in a position wherein he can be saddled with a Negress for a mistress."

She gave a wistful sigh at the thought of being his mistress. She thought she might like nothing more, but she could not entertain such fanciful dreams.

"But let us not forget he is a man of singular tastes or he would not be a member here."

Terrell put her hands on her hips as she faced Sarah. "Are you intending to fan the flames of a hope that cannot be realized? It is one thing to keep devilish secrets here at the Red Chrysanthemum, but quite another, with all that he has at stake, to consider taking a blackamoor for a mistress."

At Sarah's silence, Terrell wished she had not spoken so severely. Sarah was the closest she had ever come to having a friend in England.

"I'm sorry," Sarah said. "It only seemed that, with Master Gallant, he is…well, you know him better than I."

"In the carnal sense."

They both smiled.

"You've caught yourself a cold?" Terrell asked when Sarah wiped at her nose.

"I pray it is but a common cold and one of short duration. I had hoped to take Georgie for a walk about the park before the weather becomes colder, but my head feels as if it were stuffed with cotton."

"I can take Georgie."

"Would you?"

Glad for the chance to atone for her earlier sternness, Terrell exclaimed, "Of course!"

She reached for the only shawl she owned, ecru in color, short and with several strings coming undone.

"Take mine," Sarah offered. "If you are wearing your blue dress, this will suit nicely."

She held out a cashmere shawl with paisley trim and tasseled fringes. Terrell caressed its softness between her fingers.

"It is beautiful."

She draped it about her arms and the ends of the shawl nearly grazed the floor.

"It belonged to my mother," said Sarah.

"Then I could not. What if it came to harm while in my possession?"

"I have little occasion to wear it. When I am out, I prefer not to be noticed."

"But—"

"I insist. It is of little use in the drawer."

Dressed in her best garments and with Sarah's shawl, Terrell felt ready to appear before an assembly of the *ton*. Only her bonnet with its worn ribbons did not suit. Terrell resolved to pass by a store that sold lace and notions.

Scooping up the babe, she proceeded downstairs.

"Good day to you, Miss Terrell," Baxter greeted, his countenance betraying his appreciation.

"Good day, Baxter," Terrell replied. "I require the pram Miss Sarah keeps in the stables."

He bowed as if addressing a proper lady. "As you wish."

With George in the pram, she set out for St. James'. It was a fair walk, and a brisk wind blew at them, but she welcomed the exercise and fresh air. She had not yet reached the end of the block when she passed by Sophia and Lydia, who had also taken themselves out. She said nothing to the women as they walked by.

"Where did she come by such a lovely shawl?" Terrell heard Lydia remark.

"Pilfered no doubt," Sophia sniffed. "Blackamoors would pluck the teeth out of a dead man's mouth."

In far too good a mood to be vexed by the likes of Sophia, Terrell continued on, pushing the pram made of wicker. For the day, she could pretend that George was hers, though he was fair with flaxen hair. Back in Barbados, however, she had seen black mothers give birth to pale babies. Despite his mother's precarious situation, George looked remarkably healthy compared to the small and thin babies of slave mothers, yet no matter how sickly and emaciated the slave babies might look, they pulled upon an instinct deep inside all women.

Perhaps, Terrell thought to herself, if she were to become a courtesan who could command a tidy income, she could have Sarah and George come live with her. George would be a beloved nephew to her, for he was surely the closest she would ever come to having a child of her own.

Smiling at the boy she pulled the cover atop the pram to protect him from the wind.

Chapter Twenty-Seven

It is well-written," Sir Canning remarked, returning the letter to Charles. "It discourages but in such humble fashion that Lord Amherst cannot be but grateful for your insight. To support an envoy to China at this time is impossible. We cannot spare the resources to equip Amherst, or anyone, with the grandeur necessary to impress the emperor."

Charles gazed out the office window onto Whitehall Street below. "We could double the riches of the Macartney envoy, gift carriages encrusted with rubies and emeralds, bring golden telescopes and the finest instruments of our knowledge, and we should still fail to impress China. I made it plain in my letter that we should not be granted an audience lest we are willing to *kowtow* before the emperor. While I do not know Amherst well, he does not strike me as someone who would willingly bow to anyone but our king."

"Would *you*?"

Charles turned to his employer. "Would I what?"

"Perform this *kowtow* business."

"I would not travel thousands of miles with a ship full of our most impressive offerings to return empty-handed—or worse, with a ship full of gifts we were not given the opportunity to present."

"To require an Englishman to kneel before a sovereign not our own goes against the grain, would only demonstrate weakness, and give the Chinese emperor more reason to think our country inferior."

"China will believe herself the superior regardless of what we do. Her very name, Middle Kingdom, speaks to the position she esteems herself to occupy."

"Middle Kingdom?"

"The kingdom that exists between heaven and earth."

From his chair at his writing table, Canning appraised Charles. "I suppose if and when we entertain sending another envoy to China, the proper person to lead such an effort would be you."

Charles straightened. Ever since his father had returned home from China and described the strange and awesome country, Charles had been intrigued. He had often pondered how England could win over the might and mystery of China.

"I should be humbled by such an opportunity," he replied. Though he knew such an undertaking would not happen for years to come, the prospect was alluring.

"When you are elected to Parliament, your appointment would be a natural consideration. But perhaps your skills would be better suited to Foreign Secretary of State."

Sir Canning had alluded to this possibility before, if he should become Prime Minister.

"I think Sir Arthur will be ready to make his full commitment to you when he returns," Canning added.

"He may not wish to."

"Why would he not?"

"I cannot serve under the thumb of another man."

Canning was quiet for a moment before responding, "I think Sir Arthur would respect your autonomy."

To Charles, Canning did not sound convinced by his

own statement.

"Besides," the older man continued, "he has…"

"A handful of puppets already," Charles supplied. "I intend no disregard to Sir Arthur, but he is not a man whose generosity is not without purpose."

"That is to be expected. You ought repay his support in some fashion."

"I doubt the exchange he expects would suit my conscience."

"But you cannot hope to win without his support. I know you seek the endorsement of the Brentwoods, but if Sir Arthur backs another candidate, you are not assured victory. The burgess might go to Mr. Laurel! Consider the situation with care, Charles."

Charles obliged his employer, though he had given the matter much consideration already. As he strolled through St. James' Park, he contemplated once more the ways in which he might maintain his integrity while indebted to Sir Arthur, but found no satisfactory resolution. Heretofore he had not refused the possible endorsement of Sir Arthur, out of deference to Sir Canning and because of his own keen desire to win election. But his wariness of Sir Arthur had only grown since coming across him at the Inn of the Red Chrysanthemum. He would accept the support of Sir Arthur only if he could serve freely and vote in accordance with his own judgment.

"Oh!" a young woman cried out.

He saw a bonnet lifted by the wind and tumbled into the murky waters of the canal, out of reach. To his surprise, he recognized the woman.

"Miss Terrell," he greeted upon his approach.

She turned around, and he was struck by how lovely she looked in the light of day. He had only seen her by candlelight or moonlight before. In gloves and a shawl far too fine to be paired with her faded blue gown, she managed to look quite fetching.

"Mast—er, Mister Gallant," she returned and bobbed a quick curtsy as she brushed at the tendrils that had come undone and now whipped across her face.

He looked at her bonnet, half sunk in the water. Even with his walking stick, he would be unable to retrieve it. "Alas, I fear your bonnet lost."

Following his gaze, she pursed her lips. "Yes. I would not wish for its return, but it is my only bonnet."

Seeing the pram and George beside it, he asked, "And where is Miss Sarah?"

"Back at the inn. She nurses a cold."

"I am sorry to hear it. I pray her health improves."

"I hope as well, though the greedy part of me has thoroughly enjoyed having Georgie to myself."

They watched George, his hand upon the pram, take a step. Not too far from him, a duck waddled by. He reached a hand toward the bird.

"Georgie liked the pelicans," she said, "though I find them rather frightful creatures."

He chuckled. "Their long beaks do appear menacing."

George took another step and released his hold of the pram. Miss Terrell breathed in sharply. George wavered, then took another step, and wavered once more before falling on his arse.

"Miss Sarah will be thrilled!" Miss Terrell cried. "No, she will be cross that she missed bearing witness to his first step! I should return him. He ought not be out in such elements."

Before she could pick up George, a curl blew into her mouth. She pulled it out and replaced George in the pram.

"Do you often take solitary walks in the park, Mas— Mr. Gallant?" she asked.

"The Foreign Office is at Whitehall, not far from here, but you have come a long way, Miss Terrell."

"I am accustomed to being out of doors, and physical exertion does not disturb me."

The wind was making a fine mess of her hair. He tucked a few loose tendrils behind her ear. "You are in need of a bonnet, Miss Terrell."

She glanced at the canal where her bonnet floated and seemed to consider how to fetch it.

"Come, there are shops a block from here," he said.

"I have but three farthings upon me."

"I have enough in my purse."

She looked once more from him to her bonnet.

"Even if we could retrieve your bonnet," he allowed, "it would be quite the chore to cleanse it."

"Very well," she agreed and took the handle of the pram.

They walked a few minutes in quiet till George grew restless in the pram. Miss Terrell took him into her arms. Charles took the pram. They must have presented quite the sight: a young, unchaperoned woman with a babe strolling alongside a gentleman pushing a pram. If he should come across an acquaintance, brows would rise. Strangers might assume he was the father and she the child's nursing maid.

"I think him hungry," Miss Terrell said.

They stopped by a bakery, where he purchased hot cross buns for them both. Food in hand, George was content to return to the pram. Charles pushed the pram as Miss Terrell devoured the bun. He thought perhaps she had not had breakfast but then remembered she had partaken amply of the meal he had had prepared for her.

As if reading his mind, she said, "Back in Barbados, if you didn't eat your food fast enough, it would surely be stolen from you."

He pressed his lips into a grim line. It pained him to think of her hungry, especially as a child. He had seen many a half-starved child in China and even here in England, and it was never an easy sight.

They passed by a millinery shop, and he saw her eyes light up at the caps and bonnets on display in the window. He smiled to himself.

"A simple one will do," she said, though her eyes fixed upon one with ostrich plumes and braided trim.

He held the door for her and the pram.

"Here, what do you mean by coming in here?" the shopkeeper, a thin, older man, demanded. Upon seeing Charles, his demeanor changed. "Welcome, sir. May I be of service?"

"We wish to purchase a bonnet," Charles explained to the now thoroughly perplexed shopkeeper, who clearly did not know what to make of them, or Miss Terrell in particular, with her faded gown and elegant shawl.

But as Charles was evidently a gentleman, the shopkeeper could only respond with politeness. He looked over Miss Terrell. "Is the bonnet for her?"

"You do not expect I shall wear it?" Charles returned.

The shopkeeper colored. "Of course. Do you see one of interest? We have several charming capotes that are new."

"That one will do," Miss Terrell murmured, speaking of a capote made of linen. The crown was pleated, but the headdress lacked trimmings of any kind. It would suit a Quaker.

Charles came upon her and asked in a low voice, "Are you certain? This one is rather plain."

She nodded. She seemed unsure of herself, timid even. Quite unlike the brazen temptress he knew at the Red Chrysanthemum.

"It'll be cheapest," she replied.

"I can afford better."

"I'm certain you can, but…"

Her lower lip fell, and it was all he could do not to capture it in his mouth. From the corners of his eyes, he saw that the shopkeeper stood a respectable distance.

She whispered, "You do not mean to gift me a bonnet?"

"Why not? You've no money on you."

"But I can repay you when we are—" She looked over at the shopkeeper. "When next we meet."

"Consider it an advance on good behavior."

Her eyes widened, and he was struck by their depths. He stayed his cock by glancing over at the pram. Having finished his bun as well, George now lay upon his side and sucked his thumb.

"Why do you not look about more?" he urged Miss Terrell.

"Truly?"

He smiled at the excitement in her voice.

"Our good man has an impressive selection."

He stepped aside and watched her peruse the variety of hats.

"May I interest you, sir, as well?" the shopkeeper asked.

Content to watch Miss Terrell, Charles shook his head.

"This one, I think," she declared after she had circled the shop once. "If you approve."

She had chosen a straw bonnet with a wide brim and a

short crown. A tri-colored ribbon wound over the flat of the crown and circled its base. It was far from the fanciest bonnet but elegant in its simplicity.

"You must put it on," he said.

Standing before a looking glass, she placed the bonnet over her head and tied the ribbons beneath her chin. He had known it would look lovely upon her, and it did.

"Quite charming," he said, then turned to the shopkeeper. "Do you not agree?"

"A splendid choice."

"I meant the lady."

The man flushed. "Of-Of course."

Deciding not to tease the poor man any further, he paid for the bonnet and they went on their way. Miss Terrell appeared relieved to leave the store.

"I shall repay you," she told him, "in coin or...other ways. Whichever you prefer, Master Gallant."

A shiver went through his groin at her last two words. Damn. He would have a hard time concentrating this afternoon.

"There is no repayment necessary, Miss Terrell. Wear the bonnet in good health."

He thought he saw the glimmer of affection in her eyes as she looked at him. The bonnet suited her, the brim forming a halo about her curls, the bow adorably large beneath her chin. He could not right her past sufferings with the purchase of a bonnet, but he was gratified to provide her something that delighted her.

"Thank you," she said, her voice quivering slightly.

He inclined his head, and were they not in the middle of a street lined with shops and people, he would have pulled her into his arms and kissed her. Instead, feeling the time of his next engagement near, he took out his pocket watch. Alas, their time had passed too swiftly. He would have liked to accompany her back to the inn.

"I should return Georgie. He will want his mother when he wakes."

He paused, then decided, "You ought have accompaniment."

"I can walk fine on my own."

"You have a babe with you."

"I will let no harm come to Georgie."

Her eyes flared and he glimpsed the panther that would unfurl should anyone dare approach with malicious intent.

"My horse is not stabled far. I could accompany you and Georgie, then ride back."

"Do you not have an engagement?"

"I will tell Sir Canning to delay—"

"No. You've far more important things to do than chaperone a blackamoor and child."

He was taken aback by her blunt refusal. "Do you forget your place, Miss Terrell?"

"We're not at the Red Chrysanthemum, Mister Gallant." Her eyes glimmered. She was clearly enjoying her freedom to rebuke him. "You bought the bonnet for me. I'll take nothing more from you."

He hesitated still. She closed the distance between them and stood with her body an inch away. His pulse quickened. She could not stand in such proximity without his body crying out for her touch.

Her voice was low and ripe with desire. "But I promise to return the favor with my best behavior."

He inhaled sharply as the blood rushed to his groin. He was tempted to comment that such promises were easily broken, especially by the likes of her. Or perhaps any woman. Miss Greta had been unable to keep promises as well.

He desperately wanted to clasp her to him and kiss her. Perhaps he should have allowed her the plain capote, for then she would look far less alluring.

But he had a strange sensation that they were being watched.

She stepped away, allowing the air to return to him. "Till tonight, Master Gallant."

Composing himself, he bowed over her hand. "Till tonight then, Miss Terrell."

She curtsied. For a woman who had been a field slave, she had acquired the graces of a lady most impressively. And he was pleased to treat her as such.

He watched her walk away, dissatisfied that he had granted his work precedence over Miss Terrell. He had much to do, to be sure, and less time due to his added responsibility of the Red Chrysanthemum.

With Miss Terrell out of sight, he turned and headed back to Whitehall.

Chapter Twenty-Eight

Unsettled till he was assured that Miss Terrell and George had arrived safely at the Red Chrysanthemum, Charles concluded his meeting early and rode his horse to the inn. Upon arriving, he found no one to stable his horse at first, and instead of being greeted by Baxter, he was met by Wang, who seemed to have a sixth sense for when his employer was near.

Accustomed to being at the inn when there were patrons about, the place felt quiet to Charles, save for a surprising clamor coming from downstairs—most likely the kitchen. Charles was handing Wang his gloves when a woman screamed. The men exchanged glances.

"I will see to the horse," Wang said.

Charles made quick strides toward the kitchen and servants' quarters. He came across Miss Sarah, who had just descended the stairs into the hall. She had George in her arms.

"Master Gallant, I thought I heard someone cry out," she said.

"You best stay here," he advised.

As he neared the kitchen, he heard Baxter calling out, "Miss Terrell, please! Miss Sophia!"

"Look what you've hussies done! I bought that flour but yesterday!"

He heard the clank of falling objects and came into the

kitchen to see Miss Terrell and Miss Sophia locked together, rolling along a table. Flour had spilled all over the floor. The cook busied herself moving items away from the wrestling pair. Tippy and Lydia stared with dropped jaws. Baxter made gestures as if desiring to separate the women but not wanting to touch them. Jones leaned against a table, laughing as the women tumbled to the ground. Upon seeing Charles, however, he straightened.

Charles strode over and yanked Miss Terrell off Miss Sophia by the waist before she began pommeling the latter. Miss Terrell kicked and tried to wrench herself free, but he kept his hold on her.

"*Crazy darkie!*" Miss Sophia shrieked.

"Sow!" Miss Terrell returned, still struggling to free herself.

"Nigger-whore!"

"Stop this!" Charles barked.

Just then, Miss Sophia screamed loud enough to ring everyone's ears. Upon the ground was a fistful of her hair.

"You owe more than that!" Miss Terrell shouted.

Miss Sophia picked up her hair and began to bawl.

"Jones," Charles directed, "take Miss Terrell to Madame's chambers."

"She did it on purpose!" Miss Terrell exclaimed as Jones manhandled her out of the kitchen. "On purpose."

"The wretch!" Miss Sophia sobbed. "The miserable wretch!"

Charles looked to Lydia. "Take Miss Sophia to her quarters and comfort her."

"I've no time to go back to the market today," the cook lamented after Miss Sophia's wails could no longer be heard.

"Baxter can take a horse and ride to the market,"

Charles offered.

"Not in time for me to make the meat pies!"

"The meat pies can wait till the morrow. I am certain you can fix a worthy dinner with the hours left."

"I suppose."

"But first, what prompted the brawl between Miss Terrell and Miss Sophia?"

"I do not think they have ever taken to one another," Tippy said.

"Clearly."

"I was preparing the ingredients for my pie shells," said cook, "and telling Miss Sophia and Miss Lydia that I suspect they took some wine they ought not have, when Miss Terrell comes in, furious as the devil, and throws herself upon Miss Sophia."

"Have you any notion as to what may have caused their quarrel?"

Everyone shook their heads.

"As Miss Tippy said, they are not friendly toward one another," said Baxter. "It is fortunate you came when you did. I worried they would come to great harm. Or, at least, Miss Sophia would. Blackamoors can be hot-blooded creatures and easily excitable. Shall I go to the market now?"

"Please do."

Charles rubbed his temples. He thought of checking in on Miss Sophia, but she was likely still vulnerable to hysterics. He would deal with Miss Terrell first.

In Joan's chambers, he found Miss Terrell siting in the anteroom, her arms crossed petulantly over her chest. Across the room, Jones stood guard. Charles dismissed the muscular Negro, then turned his full attention upon the remaining blackamoor. Flour dusted her dark curls, which had come undone from its coiffure, and her gown, which now had a tear at its hem.

"What the devil prompted you to attack Miss Sophia?" he demanded.

Miss Terrell fumed. "She did it on purpose!"

"Did what?"

"Ruined the shawl!"

"The one you wore today?"

"Yes! I had placed it upon a chair as I was in a hurry. Georgie was fussing sorely. When I returned to retrieve the shawl, it was covered in *wine*. And I had seen Miss Sophia with a glass when I come in."

"But you did not see her spill the wine upon the shawl."

"I know she did it!"

"I grant it is despairing to have so pretty a shawl of yours spoiled—"

"It wasn't mine. It was Sarah's! She let me borrow it, and now it is ruined!"

"I see. I understand that is a greater pain, but what did Miss Sophia say when you approached her, or had you already judged her guilty and proceeded to tear her hair?"

"She would not admit to it. She's a cowardly sow."

"Miss Terrell, even if Miss Sophia were guilty of the crime you accuse her of, I cannot condone violence as the solution. Did you not promise me good behavior?"

Her face fell, but she defended herself by saying, "To you, Master Gallant. Miss Sophia deserves not—"

"Did I not express this morning that you should behave yourself in my absence?"

"You did."

"And what is the consequence of defying me?"

"I will be punished. But Miss Sophia owes Sarah a new

shawl!"

"I am not here at present to address Miss Sophia's wrongs, but yours, Miss Terrell."

She sat at attention. "I would be pleased to accept your punishment, Master Gallant."

Of course she would. He looked about the room and went to remove a sash from the curtains. He fit the damask over her eyes and tied the ends behind her head.

"I have a few items to collect," he said, and, taking her hand, placed it between her legs, "but you may pleasure yourself while you wait."

"Yes, Master!"

She began petting herself. After finding three of the implements he sought, he returned to the room to find Miss Terrell blushing with arousal. Her hand was now beneath her skirts. For a few minutes, he watched her, his cock stiffening at the sight of her parted lips, the sound of her purring moans.

Steeling himself, he stood before her. "Spread your legs atop the arms of the chair."

She did as told, pulling back her skirts to present him an unobstructed view of her cunnie. Desire throbbed in his veins at the sight of the dark brown folds garnished with black curls. He knelt before her and pressed his thumb to her growing clit. She drew in a sharp breath. With his thumb, he rolled the nub of flesh. Her moans grew in length. He fondled the clit as he keenly watched the evidence of pleasure waving over her countenance.

Lowering himself, he applied his tongue to her. She gasped.

"Oh, Master," she groaned.

He licked and flicked his tongue at the sensitive pearl, coaxing it to swell. He caressed her folds till her wetness flowed and she squirmed in the chair.

"Master, may I have your cock?"

"Shhh. I want only for you to submit to your punishment," he said.

Her brow furrowed. Undoubtedly she wondered how this was a punishment.

Taking her clit into his mouth, he sucked. The little bud was now nicely engorged. He had in his hand a silver clip with rounded beads. She gasped when he applied the clip to her pleasure bud. He caressed the clip and the captured flesh, eliciting more groaning. He looked at the moisture glistening upon her and took up his second item, a plug for the anus. He coated the cone of the plug by dipping it into her cunnie, then touched the tip to her nether hole.

"Yes," she breathed.

Gently, he pressed the plug into the puckered hole. At first it resisted, but the plug was one of the smaller variants of its kind. She panted when the widest part of the cone stretched her, but the hole soon swallowed the plug till only the handle, adorned with a false ruby, protruded. Her head hung over the back of the chair, and her hands rested atop her knees.

She looked beautiful.

He fondled the clip, then dipped a finger into her slit. His cock shifted as her wet heat encased his digit. He worked his finger till her brow furrowed and her legs trembled, but knowing this to be her punishment, she refrained from spending. He inserted a second finger and put his thumb at her clit. His ministrations caused her to writhe as pleasure assaulted her.

She grasped the arms of the chair. "Oh, please, oh, Lord."

Slowly, he withdrew his hand. "You may remove your

blindfold, Miss Terrell. I have one last accessory for you."

She sat up and pulled away the sash. Her look of anticipation fell into a frown as she beheld the item in his hand—a chastity belt.

"On your feet," he directed.

She rose from the chair with obvious aversion. He turned her around, bent her over the chair, and threw her skirts above her waist. The ruby winked at him from her arse. He grunted in appreciation of such delectableness before fitting the belt upon her and locking it in place.

"Need you have chosen one so cumbersome?" she asked after he had pulled her skirts back down and permitted her to stand.

"Consider," he said, "your punishment has hardly begun."

Her lips drew into a pout, and he succumbed to what he had desired to do all afternoon. He pulled her into him and crushed his mouth atop hers. She clung to his arms in surprise as he devoured lips, tongue, cheeks. God. A man should never have to crave a woman with such ferocity. It hardly felt natural. He clasped both sides of her head to hold her still so that he could indulge in the kiss with unrestrained ardor. When at last he released her, she appeared dazed.

"I have a dinner engagement this evening," he told her after his own breath had calmed, "but will leave the key with Wang if you require the plug removed to attend a bowel movement. When you are done, he can assist in replacing it."

She looked ready to scowl at him.

"Till tonight, Miss Terrell."

He left in search of Wang for his hat and gloves, but stopped first by the room of Miss Sophia.

He found the young woman had recovered from her trauma, though her eyes were still puffy from crying. Miss Lydia had remained with her and sat beside her in bed.

"I did no wrong!" Miss Sophia protested to him. "That hellcat will lie about anything!"

"It was wrong of her to accuse you when it might have been an accident," he allowed.

"Indeed! It was a simple accident, but that darkie will only believe the worst in people."

"The shawl belonged to Miss Sarah, so you will need to arrange any recompense with her."

Her eyes grew wide. Apparently she had not known the true owner of the shawl, or she had not thought she would have to atone for the mishap.

He came across Wang in the foyer and handed the valet a small key.

"Miss Terrell may require it," he explained. "I will see to my horse myself."

Wang took the key without question and handed Charles his hat and gloves. Taking his leave, Charles considered the hours before his return. The Dempseys were hosting a dinner in his honor and with the purpose of solidifying further support for him. It was not a function he could leave early. Miss Terrell would be unhappy for several hours awaiting his return. And as with any punishment with Miss Terrell, it seemed he would not be unscathed. Not when his body burned for hers.

The Chinese had many herbs to increase a man's vigor and fertility. He reminded himself to ask Wang if there was an herb that could calm desire and cool one's ardor.

Chapter Twenty-Nine

"Oh my," Sarah murmured with condolence as she eyed the metal contraption enclosing Terrell's pelvis.

Terrell dropped her skirts. "And he does not expect to return till after dinner! I pray it is an early dinner."

"I did not think Master Gallant could be so wicked."

Terrell did. Admittedly, she was drawn to this quality in him. She sat down on her bed but could not close her legs in comfort, the moisture between her flesh and the metal belt a reminder of her body's unmet desires.

"But I suppose it *was* rather bad that you tore out Sophia's hair."

"On account of your shawl!" Terrell objected.

"If Madame had been here, she would have charged you at least a sixpence for your actions."

Terrell supposed she would choose the chastity belt over paying a sixpence. She would suffer whatever Master Gallant wished to do to her.

"He has not, I think, imposed a punishment upon Sophia, and *she* started it!" Terrell looked down. "I tried to wash the shawl as best I could. Alas, the stain persists."

"Wine is dreadfully difficult to remove."

Terrell put her head in her hands. "I should never have borrowed your shawl."

Sarah put a hand upon her shoulder. "The shawl no

longer has a place in my wardrobe."

"It matters not, Lady Sarah. It was a beautiful shawl! You could have fetched a decent sum if you ever decided to sell it. Sophia should at least buy you a new one!"

Sarah scooped up George off the bed. "Perhaps she will."

"She won't lest compelled. She is not the generous sort."

"I do not know her well enough to agree or disagree."

"You tend to think kindly of people."

"I protest. I consider myself a good judge of character."

"But you are so trusting!"

"Of you. Of Master Gallant. While I will not think ill of someone without evidence, few others have my trust as completely as you do."

Terrell felt her heart twist. She blurted, "I will replace your shawl if Sophia does not. I ought never have borrowed it, but I was vain."

"Let us talk of it later. It is time for dinner."

Terrell looked at Sarah, so forgiving and gracious. She could never aspire to such qualities, nor would she try, but she admired them in Lady Sarah.

"I could not sit at the table while wearing this bloody thing," Terrell replied. She thought longingly of the food she was foregoing.

"I shall bring a plate to you then."

"You are good to me."

"As you have been to me and Georgie."

After Sarah had departed with George, Terrell reached beneath her skirts and pulled at the lock. She had tried it before and was little surprised to find it still secure. With a groan, she fell back onto her bed. She clenched the muscles between her thighs, seeking release for the tension he had stoked in her earlier. Her only solace was the fullness in her arse. But she wanted more. She wanted those Chinese balls. She wanted to stroke herself.

She could think herself to spending, but the climax would be small. And she was not permitted to spend without his permission. Granted, he would not know. Or would he? Was she capable of deceiving him or could he discern her lie as well as he discerned her arousal?

She ought not risk his displeasure. What if he made her wear the chastity belt for days? The thought both dismayed and aroused her. She shifted her hips and tried to rub her folds against the belt. She felt the beads of the clip but it was not nearly enough.

Giving up, she found *Fanny Hill* and opened the book. She gazed at the letters and thought she recognized a few words. How wonderful it would be if she could read the novel! She liked the person of Fanny, though Terrell doubted she had ever been as innocent. If she had been, too much time had passed for her to recognize any possession of it. Terrell hoped Fanny would find happiness, just as she hoped she could.

But what she thought would have made her happy was changing.

A sound at the door signaled that Sarah had returned with food, but when Terrell opened the door, she found Wang.

"Come."

The valet was decidedly not a man of many words, Terrell concluded. She followed him with equal loquaciousness. He led her to Madame Devereux's chambers and indicated she should sit in the anteroom. He placed a tray upon the table before her and poured her a cup of tea, the same blend from the night before. With a frown, she took in the small plate of apples—or possibly pears—and what appeared to be crackers covered in black seeds.

"Sarah was to bring me dinner," she said.

"This is your dinner," Wang answered, handing her the cup of tea.

"Is starvation to be part of my punishment?"

"Eating overmuch can bring on lethargy."

She accepted the cup of tea and tried a slice of apple or pear. The fruit had the crispness of apple and the sweetness of pear.

"Slowly," Wang said as she reached for her second slice.

She picked up a cracker next and scratched at a seed. "What is this?"

"Black sesame."

She tried the cracker. It was not particularly to her liking, but she finished it.

"Do you like it here in London?" she asked when it became clear that the valet was going to stand and watch her eat. When he did not answer, she tried, "Do you ever miss your homeland? China?"

"For what purpose?"

She inclined her head at the odd response, but it was a practical question and one she appreciated. She knew many a slave who wailed and despaired of their situations. While she allowed that no human could know a worse condition, she found the sobs of self-pity tiresome. She could not allow such despondency to settle in her or she would surely wish to kill herself, as many slaves did, particularly those who had come fresh off the ships, who had known a life of freedom before their captivity.

"I've no homeland to mourn," she said, "though my mother said that my grandmother was an African princess, but I know nothing of Africa and have no desire to venture there."

"I will return to China, upon my death, my ashes to be spread on the banks of the Yellow River. The leaves of the trees always fall back to the roots."

Stunned by the sudden verbosity, she had no reply at first. "England is still foreign to me, but it is home to me now. If I returned to Africa, who knows but that I might be captured and returned to slavery? In England, I am free."

She breathed in the words as if to remind herself of this sacred fortune. It did not matter if she should be destitute the rest of her life, she had freedom, and she would sooner die young, impoverished and free than die a slave.

Wang seemed to sense her inner thoughts. His expression softened. He went to the sideboard and returned with another one of the apple-pears. She realized she had finished all the fruit on the plate.

"Thank you," she said, touched by the gesture.

He said nothing and returned to being a statue. After she had finished her tea and light repast, she needed to visit the commode. She squirmed in her seat, feeling a bit ridiculous that she could not attend nature's call without seeking the assistance of another.

"I require the key," she said.

Wang produced it. "It stays in my possession."

She huffed. "Very well, but after you unlock the belt, I should be obliged to have some privacy."

He acquiesced. She gathered her skirts to give him access to the lock. She sighed as the belt came off and air caressed her parts. In the closet, she removed the plug from her arse, vowing she would never merit the damned chastity belt again.

Wang waited for her in the bedchamber, holding the belt and a new plug. This one had three successively larger balls strung together. Although she had enjoyed the insertion of the initial plug, she wanted relief from the fullness a little longer, especially as she knew not when Gallant would return.

Wang looked to the bed. "Lie down."

She bit back an impertinent response, for upsetting Wang would upset Gallant. Even if Gallant had not spoken of Wang with devotion, she could see the bond between the two men. She lay upon the bed.

Wang lifted her knees and flipped her skirts to her waist. She felt his finger at her clitoris. He wiggled the clip there, then stroked the little bud. Desire immediately percolated. He agitated his digit quickly against her, and she was surprised how ready she was for the fondling. She closed her eyes, imagining Gallant to be present. Leisurely, Wang coaxed the moisture to build. She knew no man whose touch was as patient as that of Wang or Gallant. Most men were in some haste to jab their fingers into her cunnie.

With her wetness flowing, Wang pressed a finger into her slit. His ministrations soon had her bowing off the bed. *Lord.* She had never felt pleasure build with such speed. Her teeth chattered as she tried to hold the intensity in check. Slowly, he removed his finger and pressed the smallest of the trio of balls into her. She focused on her erratic breath as the second ball entered her, then the third. After pulling them back out, now coated with her nectar, he pressed the smallest ball at her anus. Already loosened by the earlier plug, her arse took the first ball easily. The second one presented a mild fullness. The third one stretched her, making her gasp.

Wang then replaced the belt and locked it in place.

"More tea, Miss Terrell?" he inquired.

She stared at the canopy above. Once again, her body had been tormented to arousal, only to receive the chastity belt.

Tea. She didn't want any bloody tea. She wanted to spend but found herself saying, "Yes, please."

Turning her head, she watched Wang wash his hands at the basin before pouring her a cup of tea.

"Am I to wait for Master Gallant here?" she asked.

He had the same stoic countenance, save for a glimmer in his eyes. "Yes, Miss Terrell."

She turned to stare at the canopy again. "Thank you, Wang."

He bowed and took his leave. She grabbed her breasts and tried to pinch her nipples through her garments. It did little to relieve the tension in her body. She lay for several minutes. Every time she clenched her cunnie, she felt the balls more acutely. Perhaps she should have some tea to distract her from the aggravation of her body. Rising from the bed, she saw that Wang had placed *Fanny Hill* beside the tea. She went to pick up the book. She would learn to read. Equiano, a former slave, had taught himself to read and write. He had written an entire memoir, and she would read it someday.

An hour later, Wang returned and set a tray of tea upon the writing table. It must have been for Master Gallant, which meant he was arrived.

"You are to undress," Wang informed her.

Happy to have Master Gallant returned, she rose to her feet. With Wang's assistance, she divested all her garments till she stood naked but for the chastity belt, her stockings and garters. Wang rolled her nipples and attached tassels to the hardened buds before again departing.

Half an hour later, she heard the door to the anteroom open. Suspecting it to be Wang, the impish part of her considered assuming a lewd position. It would amuse her to startle the man from his impassiveness. But it would not do. Especially if it was Master Gallant. She took a position on the floor upon her knees, her hands clasped behind her and her gaze cast downward.

It was Master Gallant! She could tell by the heavier tread. The door to the bedroom opened. He stopped at the threshold. Her pulse quickened.

"A welcome sight you are, Miss Terrell."

His voice held more emotion than usual, and her heart swelled.

"I behaved badly today. Forgive me, Master," she said.

"Do you regret your actions?"

"I regret that I upset you, Master."

"But not that you made Sophia cry?"

She kept her gaze averted. "In truth, no."

He approached her and took hold of a tassel. "Where did you come by these?"

She started. "Did you not request them of Wang?"

"I will have to have a word with my valet," he murmured with some amusement. "You may rise, Miss Terrell."

He went to sit at the writing table and poured himself some tea. "Miss Sophia will compensate Miss Sarah for the loss of the shawl. She does not have the money at present, but it will be garnished from her perquisites."

"That is good, Master Gallant."

She saw that he looked into his tea and seemed rather

tired, though no less dapper in his double-breasted blue coat and fitted buff-colored trousers. "Are you unwell, Master Gallant?"

"Merely a little fatigued," he replied. "My dinner was long and wearisome, availing little, though it had been heralded as an opportunity for me to meet more supporters. The occasion was more properly a chance for Mrs. Dempsey to present her daughter. The other dinner guests had little interest in the election."

Terrell quelled the rise of jealousy. "Do you need more supporters if you have the support of Sir Arthur?"

"I am not assured the support of Sir Arthur, and I am reluctant to seek it."

"But he could secure the election for you?"

"He could."

"Do you not wish to win?"

"I do. It has been my desire to become a Member of Parliament since I was a child and my father sought the burgess for Porter's Hill. I witnessed the speeches he made atop the hustings, and they always inspired such promise."

"Was he elected to Parliament then?"

"He tried. Thrice. And failed thrice. But my victory would be his victory."

"Then why do you hesitate to secure the support of Sir Arthur?"

"And entail myself in bondage to him?"

"There are worse forms of bondage."

He looked at her in compassion. "I suppose I am fortunate to have such a dilemma. It has been presented to me that Sir Arthur's support is mine for the taking if I request it."

But she saw that his brow furrowed at the prospect. Wanting to improve his mood, she approached him, kneeling before him.

"May I show you the benefits of bondage?" she inquired.

His brows rose. She placed her hands upon his knees and parted them. She settled herself between them and leaned toward his crotch.

"Wang tells me you have been good."

"I have, Master Gallant. And I wish to show you how very good I can be."

She reached for the buttons of his fall and saw movement there. He toyed with one of the tassels.

"I think Wang partial to you."

Remembering the Oriental's exquisite touch, she said, "I am rather partial to him as well."

Gallant wove his hand into her hair. "Are you?"

She thought she detected a hint of jealousy. "I could service you both, if you wished."

His hand tightened. "Jezebel."

"Only if you wished it, Master."

She caressed his erection through his trousers before returning to the buttons. He allowed her to pull back the fall. His cock protruded tall and proud. She wrapped a hand about his shaft. This would be her dinner. She would prefer it to the finest dishes prepared by the Regent's cook.

"May I taste of this fine cock, Master?"

He grunted. She placed her mouth over him and slowly slid down its length. It pulsed inside her. The taste of him, the firmness, the girth filling her mouth ignited her own desire. She wanted to devour him but sought her own patience as she bobbed her head methodically, up and down his cock, dragging her tongue along its underside. Moaning, he slumped farther into the chair. The more she took of him, the more her own arousal peaked. Holding the base of his cock, she sucked him in earnest.

"God," he breathed.

She took him deep into her throat and felt his grip twisting in her hair.

"Cease," he muttered. "We have yet to finish your punishment."

"Please let me pleasure you, Master," she murmured against his cock. "You deserve to spend."

He drew in a sharp breath as her mouth pulled at him. When he did not protest, she suckled his instrument as hard as she could. He bucked his hips a few times before bursting inside of her mouth. She swallowed every last drop, filling her belly with his seed, before allowing his cock to slip from her.

"My God," he sighed with a shake of his head.

Triumphant, she licked her lips. Happy to have brought him pleasure, she did not mind the agitation in her own loins, the moisture collecting once more against the steel, the craving between her legs.

He pulled her up to him and smothered her lips with his mouth, tasting his own mettle. She returned the kiss with desperate longing, as if pressing her tongue deep and hard into him could relieve the pressure below her navel.

Holding her, he rose to his feet, then bent her over the writing table. His fatigue gone, he leaned over her and whispered, "Let us finish your punishment now, Miss Terrell."

Chapter Thirty

Charles whipped out the key Wang had handed him earlier. Wang had said little, but the tenting at the man's crotch had said enough. Although Wang had been asked to perform rather unorthodox duties, what valet would not jump at the chance to touch a woman's cunnie? And one as delectable as Miss Terrell's.

"Did you enjoy your chastity belt, my love?" he asked as he held her against the table.

"I did."

"Did you?"

"No, but I am grateful for my punishment, Master."

Perhaps she could be a good submissive after all, he thought. He unlocked the belt from her. The scent of her arousal made his blood pound. His cock began to stir again.

He observed the ring at the end of the string of balls dangling below her shapely arse. Reaching beneath, he found her sodden. He rubbed the clip against her clitoris. She moaned. No doubt Wang had aroused her well. Before Confucius, Daoism had prevailed, as did the belief that a woman's pleasure, the essence of *yin,* was essential to the health of a man, the essence of *yang.* Charles remembered being astounded at how long Wang could sustain an erection in the brothels of Canton, and was determined to match the man. He had yet to succeed, but his forbearance had greatly improved in the effort.

He caressed Miss Terrell between the thighs till she moaned and gripped the edge of the table. He then went to retrieve a flogger.

"I had promised myself a crimson arse," he told her as he adjusted himself.

Gently, he circled the tails against one cheek, admiring how the flesh quivered beneath the slaps. He pulled at his cock and applied the flogger to her other cheek, warming the flesh.

"What is your safety word, Miss Terrell?"

"Fanny."

"Good. You will count to twenty."

"Twenty?!"

"What was that, Miss Terrell?"

"Thank you, Master. I am pleased to receive twenty lashes from you."

"Good."

He threw the tails at her backside. She grunted as the tips bit at her.

"One," she mumbled into the table.

He lashed her a little harder.

'Two!" she yelped.

He whipped her several more times before pausing to fondle her folds. He tugged at the clip and gazed at where the balls were. Tonight he would take her arse. His cock reared its head.

"Eight!" she cried.

He slapped the flogger harder upon her derriere.

"Nine," she counted through gritted teeth. "Ten!"

He paused to let the strikes sink in. Her arse had begun to blush a lovely shade of pink, but crimson was his goal.

"Eleven! Twelve!"

He set aside the flogger to remove his coat. Without Wang, the simple task took much longer, but he wanted more freedom of movement for his arms. Free of his coat, he felt between her thighs to find her wetter than before. He brushed the knuckles of a hand lightly over the curve of her rump. She shivered. Standing back, he whipped the tails where he had caressed seconds ago.

"Thirteen!"

His gaze raked over her, from the voluptuousness of her arse to her supple legs, the lower half encased in stockings. His cock had returned to life. By chance, he glanced at her mangled back and was tempted to lighten the force of his blows. But Miss Terrell was possessed of a strong body.

All the same, he asked, "What is your safety word?"

"I will reach twenty, Master Gallant. I promise you."

"Very well."

He struck her derriere without moderation.

She pressed her forehead upon the table. "Fourteen."

And again.

"Fifteen!"

She shifted her weight from one foot to the other, subtly rubbing her folds together. Reaching beneath her, he pulled off the clip and rubbed her as the blood rushed to the area. Her legs trembled as pleasure threatened to overwhelm her. Knowing she could not yet spend, she tensed her body against his fondling. She emitted a quivering moan.

Stepping back, he gave her rear a harsh lashing.

"Sixteen, seventeen!"

The flogger slapped against her. She cried out. Now the streaks across her cheeks glowed red against the darkness of her skin.

"Eighteen," she choked.

He slid his finger into the ring and drew the balls out. She quaked and her legs buckled momentarily. *Damnation.* He wanted to toss aside the flogger and fuck her without further ado. Having spent once already, he could sustain a longer congress. The thought of overwhelming her body with pleasure made his blood boil.

"Nineteen," she cried out when he applied the tails again.

He smacked her good and hard for the final count.

"T-Twenty...thank you, Master."

Setting the flogger beside her on the table, he retrieved a vial containing an oil infused with Chinese herbs. At first, he had found many of the herbs and practices of the Chinese, such as the drinking of snake's blood, to be revolting. The herbs that Wang used were often pungent or even rancid in flavor, but there were qualities, such as the youthful and flawless complexions of northern Chinese women, that suggested the traditions were not without merit.

He smoothed the oil over her to cool her burning arse. He flipped her over and rubbed the oil over her belly, through the curls at her mound, and down to her clitoris. She shivered, lust sparkling in those large, dark eyes of hers. He poured oil about her navel and spread it over her torso, making her body glisten, and cupped a breast. Putting down the vial, he kneaded both orbs, then tugged on the tassels. There was not an inch of her that he touched that did not delight his hands.

Grasping her by the legs, he lifted her rump onto the table, which caused her head to hang over the edge. He opened a drawer where he had set aside several cords of rope. Taking her right leg, he tied her right wrist to the ankle, then wrapped her elbow to her shin. He did the same to her left leg and arm. With her thighs splayed wide, her most intimate parts were on display for him. He stroked himself at the sight of those lovely folds and that teasing bud of flesh, a pearl of pink amidst the dark.

He pushed her ankles into the air, then picked up the flogger and landed the tails between her thighs. His cock throbbed at her wail.

"Hold your position," he instructed, pushing her ankles back up.

"Yes, Master," she whispered.

He flogged her mons. She cried out.

"Thank you, Master!"

Pleased that he did not have to remind her, he fondled her clitoris.

She moaned, "Oh, Master!"

He whipped at her cunnie, making her body jump and her limbs jerk. Seeing her body twitch, her belly extend and retract from her breaths, he knew it would not be long.

He stung her with the flogger one last time. She howled, her legs thrashed before she forced them back to their position. Tossing aside the flogger, he pointed his cock at her cunnie and pushed the crown inside.

Was there a vision more provocative than that of his cock buried inside her? She flexed about his tip, enticing him to sink more of his length into her. He obliged, relishing the way she gripped at him. Buried to the hilt, he reached for her breasts and manhandled them.

"Oh, yes," she murmured.

He slapped at a breast and yanked the tassel off the other. She yelped. Her cunnie flexed. He withdrew, watching his cock slide out of her slit, shiny with her moisture, then rammed himself back in. With her cunnie at his mercy, he was tempted to pound himself into her. He could punish her further by seeking his own end while denying hers, but he derived too much fulfillment from her spending to refuse her for long.

"Look at me," he commanded.

She raised her head. He grabbed her hair to help keep her head up and began a rhythmic thrusting. He wanted to see her countenance strained in pleasure. Their gazes locked as he drove his cock into her. Brow furrowed, rosy lips parted, she looked beautiful. He shoved his hips faster and harder, his pelvis slapping her bottom. The heated embrace of her cunnie would never cloy. The more his cock tasted of her, the more it desired. He rubbed her clitoris when he withdrew, leaving only the head of his shaft inside her.

"Master, you will make me spend," she pleaded.

"Then spend, my dear," he replied. "You have earned it."

Her eyes widened with hope. He slapped a breast several more times and pinched the nipple before vigorously thrusting into her. As with any man, there existed the temptation to slam haphazardly into her, especially when his cods boiled with desire, but he kept a pace and angle that would make her pleasure optimal. Her eyes rolled toward the back of her head.

"Oh, God, oh, Lord," she gasped. "Master—"

And then her body fell into spasms. Her cry resounded off the walls. Holding back the urge to follow her, he fondled her clit as he slowed his thrusting. She wailed and gasped, gasped and wailed. Her back bowed off the table and her limbs jerked. Her cunnie throbbed about his cock. A spray of moisture, a fountain of her ecstasy, followed his every thrust.

He ceased his movements as the rapture began to fade, leaving her huffing and shaking. He released her hair and her head fell back.

But he was not done. There remained one thing he wanted to do. He undid the ropes binding her, flipped her back onto her stomach and aimed his cock at her arse. He pressed the crown into her small opening and nearly spent as the tightness enveloped him.

"Oh, God," she moaned.

When he had resumed control, he slowly pushed himself farther. Her moans grew longer. Having been filled already, she was ready for his intrusion. Yet, she felt incredibly tight. Her instinct was to push out the invader. He reached around her hip and stroked her clitoris. She relaxed and soon he was able to sink his entire length into her.

"Oh, yes, fuck my arse, Master," she murmured.

Needing no further invitation, he withdrew and thrust back in, shutting his eyes to the exquisiteness clasping his cock. He rolled his hips cautiously, wanting to build her pleasure, not knowing how versed she was to anal congress. But she soon proved as ravenous as he. She wiggled her derriere at him. Grabbing her hips, he sank himself into her over and over.

"Master, may I spend again?"

"You may."

It pleased him that she enjoyed the anal penetration as much as he; pleased him that the wantonness of being fucked over the writing table did not discomfort her. Perhaps it aroused her. Perhaps she enjoyed having him use her body. And make use of her, he would.

He shoved his cock deep into her at a steady rate. She

mumbled and murmured till the incoherence turned into screams as her body convulsed once more. Unable to contain himself, he rammed into her arse, pounding her into the table until his release came as a blinding explosion. Currents shot up and down his legs as his entire body shuddered, pumping seed after seed into the depths of her bowels.

When he had emptied himself, he staggered back and fell into the chair behind him. He caught her before she slid from the table and pulled her onto his lap. She rested her head against his chest while he caught his breath and waited for the beating of his heart to return to normal. As marvelous as their coupling had been, this, too, was rewarding. Feeling her body upon his now had a calming effect, and he felt at peace, comforted by her warmth.

"Thank you, Master," she whispered.

He caught himself before suggesting that she should misbehave more often. Instead, he asked, "How fares your arse?"

"'Tis your arse now, Master Gallant. You have marked it for your own."

He drew in a sharp breath. He was not the first to venture into forbidden territory, but he did like the sound of her words. He realized then that he wanted not just her arse, but all of her. Weaving his hand into her hair, he massaged the back of her head as he contemplated the prospect of having Miss Terrell all to himself, whenever he wished. There was much he could do, more heights of pleasure and pain that he could take her to.

"Sir Arthur returns in eight days' time," he thought aloud.

"Let us not think of Sir Arthur till the time is near," she said, nestling herself into the crook of neck. "Let us enjoy our time together before it must end."

"It need not end." When she said nothing, he added, "Forsake Sir Arthur."

She was quiet at first. "I doubt Madame would approve."

"Leave Joan to me. She owes me a favor, after all."

Terrell lifted her head to look him in the eye with solemnity. "Are you in earnest?"

He felt a surprising giddiness. "I am."

Her bottom lip fell. He tightened his hold of her head. "I want you to be mine, Terrell."

Though she had not responded verbally with the excitement he had expected, the look in her eyes was enough. He crushed her lips to his. As they kissed, he knew he had spoken on impulse, but he would think through the ramifications later. For now, as she met the pressure of his mouth with her own intensity, he knew his sentiments were returned.

His last challenge at the Red Chrysanthemum had ended unfavorably, but this time, he was determined to win.

THE END

MASTER VS. TEMPTRESS:
THE FINAL SUBMISSION

Will the temptress forsake or surrender to the Master?

Though no one can take her to the erotic heights that Master Charles Gallant can, Terrell is forced to choose Sir Arthur – for her sake as well as Gallant's. Sir Arthur holds Gallant's career in his hands. Without Sir Arthur's support, Gallant will not realize his lifelong ambition to become a Member of Parliament and succeed where his father before him had failed.

When Terrell chooses Sir Arthur over him, Charles is devastated. He will be damned if he has his heart broken a second time at the Red Chrysanthemum, where members take carnal pleasures to the extreme. Charles vows to show Miss Terrell that she belongs with him by punishing her body with wicked, wanton pleasure.

But can he command the submission of her life or will love prove their ultimate devastation?

January 2016

ABOUT THE AUTHOR

EM BROWN is an award-winning multi-published author of contemporary and historical erotic romance. She found the kinky side to her writing after reading stories at Literotica.com. She likes to find inspiration from anywhere and everywhere, be it classical movies, porn, embarrassing high school photos, her favorite Sara Lee dessert, and the time she accidently flashed an audience with her knickers.

For more wicked wantonness, visit
www.EroticHistoricals.com.

CPSIA information can be obtained
at www.ICGtesting.com
Printed in the USA
LVHW020051230423
745098LV00026B/781

9 781942 822073